Return to Whittakerville

Shirley A. Roe

The Whittaker Saga continues....

RealTime Publishing
Limerick Ireland

First Printing

This is work of fiction. Any similarity to persons alive or dead is purely coincidental. All historical facts and historical characters are added purely for the reader's enjoyment and enlightenment. Any interaction with these characters is purely fiction.

ISBN: 978-1-84961-009-4

RealTime Publishing
www.realtimepublishings.com
www.theebooksale.com

Other books by Shirley A. Roe

Dreams and Nightmares: The Martha Whittaker Story
A Call to Faith and Freedom
The Whittaker Family Reunion

Acknowledgements:

A special thanks to Nancy Morris, for all of her hard word and diligence in producing the cover and to the best publisher an author could have, Richard O'Brien, RealTime Publishing.

Mothers and Daughters

"What I would like to give my daughter is freedom. And this is something that must be given by example, not by exhortation. Freedom is a loose leash, a license to be different from your mother and still be loved . . . . Freedom is . . . not insisting that your daughter share your limitations. Freedom also means letting your daughter reject you when she needs to and come back when she needs to. Freedom is unconditional love." Erica Jong

Dedication:
This book is dedicated to three very important women. My mother, Pearl who was always there to help and support me, no matter how crazy or outlandish the idea. Now our roles are reversed, I am taking care of you.

My daughter Laura, a beautiful woman both physically and spiritually who is not afraid to live her dreams and make them a reality. I hope I was instrumental in bringing that into your life. I am proud to be your mother. Live, laugh and love my lovely daughter, for the world is yours for the asking.

My granddaughter, Haley who makes me burst with pride at the intelligent, loving and beautiful woman she has become. At sixteen, your journey into womanhood is just beginning, decide what you want and then go after it with everything you have. Live your passion; life is to be lived to the fullest, every minute of every day.

I love all of you, you make me who I am and I thank you.

Dedicated to Mothers and Daughters everywhere.

St. Louis 1882

Chapter One

Anna

"I'll be right back." The pert young woman started down the aisle of the moving train. She steadied herself by clutching the seatbacks.

"Where do you think you're going?" He grabbed her arm roughly.

She wrenched her arm away from his grip, repeating sternly, "I said, I'll be right back." He glared at her with eyes as black as night. Ignoring his warning glare, she moved toward the businessman in the front of the train car, reading a copy of the St. Louis Post Dispatch. Approaching silently from behind, she casually dropped her handkerchief. As she stooped to retrieve it, her eyes scanned the headline: St. Louis Businessman escapes death at hand of kidnapper, child still missing.

The businessman turned, sensing her presence. He took in her soft chestnut hair and her deep green eyes, losing himself for a moment in her beauty; he could not ignore her great interest in the newspaper. "Would you like to read this? I am finished with it. I also have a copy of the St. Louis Daily Globe, if you would like it." She smiled up at him from her crouched position and quickly but elegantly regained her posture. From the rear of the car, dark eyes watched with great interest, his body ready to spring into action.

"Why yes, I would be very pleased to read them, if you are finished. I lived in St. Louis for sometime and I am always interested in what is happening there." She fluttered her dark lashes, taking the newspapers from his extended hand. "Thank you kindly."

Retreating quickly back to the anxious young man, she sank into the seat beside him. He clenched his teeth, “Don’t push me too far, Anna.”

“Or what? You’ll stab me like you stabbed my father? You are just lucky he is alive, according to this paper or I would have to kill you, myself.” Her voice was quiet but assertive. She sounded like she meant it.

“You, a feeble woman would kill me. Ha, don’t make me laugh. I would like to know how.” He turned toward her keeping his voice menacingly low, challenging her.

“Oh, I can kill you very easily. Just don’t fall asleep.” She sneered, glaring back at him, matching his evil stare. He hesitated, considering her statement, and then started to laugh.

“You would, wouldn’t you? Anna, you are a woman after my own heart.” The tension was broken. She joined in his laughter just as the businessman walked by.

“Newlyweds?”

“None of your….” Anna pressed her lips to Jeb’s to quiet him.

She smiled up at the gentleman, “Yes, just married, thank you.”

Jeb clenched his teeth, remaining silent until they were alone. “What did you do that for?” He leaned closer to be sure no one could hear them.

“ Mainly because a young woman can not travel alone unless chaperoned or married. According to this paper, the police are looking for some crazy Indian that kidnapped the child of a wealthy St. Louis businessman, after stabbing him with intent to kill. There is a reward.” She looked at him carefully, fixing his cravat. “You look very handsome and very civilized in my brother Ezekiel’s clothes and we don’t want to raise any suspicions. Newlyweds are much more acceptable than a ‘crazy Indian and a child’, don’t you think?”

"Alright, you are right, but why on earth is the press referring to you as a 'child'? You are seventeen, for heaven's sake." The use of the word 'child' confused him, but he was relieved that Jeremy Whittaker was alive. He had stabbed him in a fit of rage. It was never his intention to kill anyone; he just wanted what was rightfully his.

"It is better that these people think we are newlyweds. They will ignore us. If you must know, I lied to you in New York. I am only fifteen. But I will be sixteen in two months and I am hardly a 'child' as you can attest to." She squeezed his arm, wanting to return to the boisterous mood of a few moments ago. She was enjoying this grown up interaction.

"Fifteen! What have I done?" He ran his hands through his newly- cut black hair, it felt strange. He was used to wearing it much longer. He had to admit, she was clever. He thought back to the church, where he had threatened her family. He had stabbed her father and obtained a letter that would secure his future. He was shocked when Anna offered to go away with him. After leaving the scene, she convinced him to stop at her parents' mansion to get some traveling clothes. She also opened her father's safe and secured a large sum of money, which had allowed them to board this train for Wyoming. Once on the train, she cut his hair, dressed him in her brother's fine clothes and he did look very different. He still could not believe she had come willingly. She was definitely an asset, but fifteen! He had not touched her sexually since they had left St. Louis. But, there had been that trip to New York when they first met, months ago. Jeb was still convinced she was too drunk to remember exactly what happened and he intended to keep it that way. His head was in his hands, his face filled with dread.

"Oh, stop being so dramatic. People always call me Sarah Bernhardt, but you are being much more melodramatic than I ever was. Now sit up and act like we're newlyweds. She moved into his lap. He tensed; his whole body was on edge under her touch. His skin burned, his desire was growing stronger. She snuggled her head under his chin. *Oh Lord, help me stay strong,* was all he could think of.

"I would rather hear what that newspaper has to say. Read it to me." He gently but firmly nudged her off of his knee, much to his own relief.

"Oh, fine but you are getting to be a bore. That's why I left St. Louis. My family was so boring." She pouted as she picked up the newspaper and began to read. "Wealthy business owner, Jeremy Whittaker is recovering from stab wounds. Mr. Whittaker and his family were attending the marriage of their son, Abraham Whittaker to Miss Vivienne LaRue, when a crazed Indian savagely attacked Mr. Whittaker. Before the suspect left the scene, their child was taken captive. The man was last seen riding out of St. Louis with Anna, the daughter of Jeremy and Martha Whittaker. Martha Whittaker is the owner of St. Louis Haute Couture. Mr. Whittaker is expected to survive, however he will be convalescing for some time. Mr. Austin Wells, the general manager, has taken charge of the St. Louis Import/Export business. The Whittakers have offered a large reward for information leading to the location and safe return of Anna."

"So I am a crazed Indian? No mention of the fact that I am the son of Jeremy Whittaker's dead brother? No mention of why I was there? Just a crazy Indian who stabs him for no reason and then steals a child? What kind of bull is this?" He snatched the paper from her hands. Not being able to read himself, Jeb had to trust her to tell him the truth. He was furious. He threw the papers to the floor and stomped out of the railcar. She watched him go, making sure she smiled at the other passengers. Luckily they were seated some distance away and had not heard the conversation.

"Lover's spat," she announced to no one in particular. Anna calmly picked up the papers, Jeb's bowler hat and followed him. Sympathetic, understanding nods from the other passengers greeted her as she passed. Anna's fine clothes and sophistication made her appear much older than fifteen. She raised no suspicion.

Back in their sleeper, Jeb fumed. He paced back and forth in the tiny space. She opened the door. Having grown used to his temper in the short time they had been together, she remained silent. He punched the bed hard with his fist; his whole body shook. "I will never be anything more than a crazy Indian. You can dress me up and call me by my white man's name, but no one will ever respect me." Anna knew that Jeb had a very bad temper, she let him vent for a few minutes. Slowly she moved toward him, she pulled him into her arms and held him. At first his body was stiff, but soon, uncharacteristically, he began to tremble. His arms gripped her tightly; his body shook as he struggled to regain control. They remained like that for several minutes.

"I want you to sit down and listen to me, Jeb. Newspaper reporters love to use words that will tantalize the reader. They often leave out details to make the story more interesting and exciting. That said, I want to talk about us. No, don't interrupt me." She put her hand on his shoulder to comfort him. It also quieted him, allowing her to continue. "You are the son of a man that had a town named after him, granted he was a bastard, but he was still famous. I know you hate him and hold my family responsible for your life of poverty and cruelty. But, my family honestly did not know you existed." He started to interrupt her, "That is another story, Jeb. Now back to your father and the town that is his namesake. We can use that to our advantage. You and I are going to travel as man and wife to Whittakerville, Wyoming; where you will claim the money that represents your inheritance. Money has power. Trust me, I have lived in the lap of luxury all of my life and

I know what kind of power money holds. You look suave and sophisticated in Zeke's European designer clothes. By the time we get to Whittakerville, I will teach you to sign your name and to read a little."

"By the time we get there! I can't read or write at all, it will take longer than that. Besides, I agree with you; money is power but respect is what I want." He was about to stand and exit the car. She held on to him, applying just the slightest pressure to his arm as he stood up.

"Listen to me, I am not finished. I don't know why, but I care for you. I really do. I have always been attracted to you and I see you as my ticket out of St. Louis and on to bigger and better things. I want to be free, Jeb. You and I can be free. We will have money; we will make you into a man who everyone will respect. Your Indian halfbreed past will disappear and you will be the white son of Jebediah Whittaker, founder of Whittakerville. Your father was a bastard who beat his family. He even beat your mother." He bristled at the mention of his mother, who was the unwilling squaw mistress of Jebediah Whittaker. Anna continued, "He still had the respect of everyone in the town. He was the beloved pastor of the church. No one knew who he really was. You can do this, Red. You can do this." He looked at her with such wanting in his eyes. He wanted to believe her. He wanted to be the man she described. Insecurity made him wonder, *Is it possible? Can I do this?*

"Careful, you just called me Red; it's Jeb from now on, remember?" He took a deep breath and tried to calm himself. "That was quite a speech. Next thing you'll be telling me you "love" me." He challenged her sarcastically, but held his breath waiting for her answer. *Do I want you to love me, Anna?*

"No." She almost shouted. "Let's get this straight. I 'love' no one. Love makes you weak. Love makes people do things they don't want to do. People say they love you but they never prove it. I will never be weak. I will never ‘love’ anyone but myself. I said I care for you.” She stopped to take a breath. He stared at her. She was a curiosity. Anna stared at the floor composing herself. He was amazed at how quickly she could control her emotions and take on a completely different persona.

“Now are you ready to start learning to write your name? No time like the present. You are my challenge and I’m ready to make you into Jeb Whittaker, gentleman.” She took paper and pencil from her bag and motioned for him to sit beside her. She wrote large letters on the page. Disappointed in her answer, he took the pencil from her hand. He didn’t understand how she could calm him the way she did. She had a power over him that no human being had ever had. The clickety-clack of the rails and the sound of the train whistle disappeared into the background as Red Fox, put pencil to paper and shakily printed, J E B, for the first time in his life.

Chapter Two

Back in St. Louis

"Austin, I am worried about Martha. She has not been the same since Jeremy was stabbed. The poor thing is under such pressure, trying to care for him, take care of the shop and still have time for her sons and their families. She is going to make herself sick." Loretta Wells paced back and forth in her lovely St. Louis home. She stopped to gaze at the white powdering of snow on the garden. The snowflakes glistened like diamonds. She barely saw them. Martha was her best friend. Loretta was very concerned for Martha's well being.

"Loretta, I have taken over all of Jeremy's responsibilities at St. Louis Import Export and you have been spending longer hours at the Haute Couture, there is only so much we can do. Now sit down and drink your tea." Austin too had been feeling the pressure. The Whittakers were a large part of their lives and he was worried about Jeremy's health. He seemed to be taking a long time to recover. It was taking its toll on all of them. He pulled his wife gently into the chair, smoothing her blonde locks with his hand. Handing her the china teacup, he turned to look out of the window. "The snow is piling up." His hand automatically went to his mustache. It was an unconscious reflex. He did it when he was worried, and had since he was very young. "I guess the police have had no word of Anna's whereabouts. I know that is a great concern for Martha and Jeremy and could be affecting his recovery."

"Don't even mention that little bitch's name to me. She went willingly with that lunatic. I would not be surprised if she planned the whole thing." Loretta had no sympathy for Anna Whittaker. Anna was responsible for the Wells' son David, having joined the navy and Loretta would never forgive her.

"Loretta, please you must stop blaming Anna. I am sure she had nothing to do with that man stabbing her father. She went with him to save the rest of us. She sacrificed herself. I think it was very noble."

"Noble! I still say she planned the whole thing. No one will ever convince me that she did it to 'save the rest of us' as you put it. We all know what a selfish, self centered little…"

"Talking about Anna again?" Abby, walked in the room, cutting off her mother's tirade. "I agree with Mother, Anna Whittaker does not do anything without an ulterior motive. I think she was in on it from the beginning and they won't find her easily. She has wanted to be away from St. Louis for months and now she has done it. Well, good riddance, I say." Austin looked from his daughter to his wife, the two were very similar in appearance and temperament; he knew there was no point in arguing with these two.

"Where is Ezekiel today? You two are usually joined at the hip." He laughed as Abby made a face at him.

"Zeke has gone out to Abe's place with Martha. She needed a break. Annabelle is sitting with Jeremy. He loves seeing the grandkids and Martha thought it would be good for him." Her love of Ezekiel shone on her face when she spoke of him. "Little Sissy is playing nurse. She had Jeremy all bandaged up with rags and was feeding him imaginary chicken soup when I left." The three of them laughed.

In another part of St. Louis, the Whittakers' mansion sat on a quiet street in upscale Vandeventer Place. The brick two-story house, with six bedrooms, a lovely sitting room, great room, full conservatory, study, kitchen and good-sized dining room sat on a large four-acre lot. It was the home Martha and Jeremy bought after their wedding almost twenty years ago. Jeremy Whittaker lay in his bed; pillows piled high behind his head. His breathing was shallow and his skin was pale. A fire burned brightly in the large fireplace. Five-year-old Sissy wrapped his hand in rags. “Now, don’t use that hand for six weeks. Do you hear me, Granddad?” He laughed and nodded his head. Sissy continued fixing his covers and muttering to herself. Her red head bobbing up and down. Just being with her and young Thomas had lifted his mood considerably.

“Chestnut is getting really good at jumping, Granddad. Aunt Viv has been teaching both of us to jump over logs and fences and we are almost ready for the spring fair. Aunt Viv says if we practice all winter we should be ready. I wish I could jump like her and Blackjack.” Jeremy smiled at his grandson. Thomas, at ten, was turning into a fine, young man. The incident in the church had matured him a great deal. It was a traumatic time for all of them but somehow Thomas felt guilty and blamed himself. He was silent for days afterward. Isaac and Annabelle were very worried about him. Abraham’s new wife, Vivienne was spending a great deal of time with Thomas and it seemed to be working.

“Take your time and listen to Vivienne, she knows what she is talking about, especially when it comes to horses.” Jeremy paused to cough. “I am glad that Chestnut came home to you, Thomas.” The mention of the horse’s return brought back memories of that dreaded day. The man that stabbed him rode off with his daughter Anna, on Thomas’ horse, Chestnut. Jeremy was very worried about his daughter.

“It was a miracle. We all thought Chestnut was gone for good and then four days later, he just walks into the barn. I am very thankful that God showed him the way home.” Thomas saw the far away look in his grandfather’s eyes. “God will bring Auntie Anna home to you, Granddad.

Have faith. Mama says that God listens to our prayers and I prayed very hard for Chestnut to come home and he did. I know Auntie Anna will come home safe and sound." Jeremy looked at Thomas; he could not speak for the lump in his throat. He reached out and patted Thomas' hand. Annabelle entered the room carrying a tray. The smell of fresh chicken soup filled the room.

"Time for Granddad's lunch." She tried to set the tray on the table beside the bed but Sissy had piled it high with nursing apparatus. "Sissy move all of your things so I can put the tray down."

"I already fed Granddad some chicken soup. Sick people are supposed to eat chicken soup." She nodded her little head in a knowing manner and Jeremy and Annabelle laughed.

"Yes, I know but imaginary chicken soup is not very filling. Now, move it!" Sissy slowly moved her things and Annabelle placed the tray on her father-in law's lap. She wiped her hands on her apron. "I want you to eat all of this. You need to build up your strength." Jeremy looked at Annabelle, her red hair piled high on her head giving height to her five- foot frame. His eyes moved to the tray, bulging with food.

"I am not a farmer like Isaac, my appetite is much smaller than his. You have enough food for all of us here. Sissy, Thomas, come and help Granddad eat all of this." The family sat with Jeremy while he ate most of his lunch. Thomas and Sissy helped themselves to fresh cookies. He soon grew tired.

"We will go downstairs and let you sleep. The doctor is coming later to check on you." Annabelle ushered the children from the room. Jeremy closed his eyes. A sharp pain shot through his side, he repositioned himself. A coughing spasm overtook him, perspiration dripped from his forehead. After a few minutes, he settled comfortably, under the covers.

Dear God, bring Anna back home to us safe and sound. I know she is impetuous but we miss her so. I need to know she is safe, please send us a message. With his prayer on his lips, Jeremy fell asleep.

Martha and Ezekiel had spent the afternoon with Abraham and Vivienne. Their newly acquired house was large. The kitchen was bright and airy with freshly painted cupboards and walls. Abraham had turned part of the house into his medical office. After his last patient left, he joined the others for tea in the kitchen. “It looks like the farm folks around here have discovered Doc Abe’s place. That was quite the crowd you had in there.” Ezekiel teased his brother.

“Don’t knock it, three patients in one day is enough to pay the bills. Besides I spend two days a week at the hospital, so we are doing very well, thank you.” Abraham smiled and winked at his wife. He and Vivienne had only been married for a short time but they fit like hand and glove. She was the best thing that had ever happened to him. “So how is Papa doing? I stopped in yesterday on my way home from the hospital and he seemed to be showing some improvement.” Martha and Ezekiel nodded. Hair perfectly coifed and wearing her latest design, in contrast, Martha’s face was showing the strain. Dark circles under her eyes told them that she was not sleeping well. “Mother, how are you feeling? You look like you need a good night’s sleep.”

“I’m fine. I just wish Jeremy would get better soon. I know that not knowing where Anna is, is putting a huge strain on him, well, on both of us. I wish she would write or come home. We need to know if she is alright.” The others looked at each other knowingly. No one was sure whether Anna went willingly to remove them from danger or whether she really wanted to go with the stranger that turned out to be her cousin, Jeb Whittaker. They were still reeling from the shock of it all. Vivienne moved over and placed her arm around Martha's shoulder. "Vivienne, you are such a blessing to us all. Annabelle told me that Thomas is absolutely beaming with joy every time you take him out to practice his jumping. He is a real horseman, that one." Vivienne smiled shyly. The young woman from Louisiana was still getting used to this large close-knit family. She often felt overwhelmed by them all and was happy to ride out on Blackjack with Thomas or go to Isaac's and help with the chores. She felt happiest working close to the land and this new life suited her perfectly. Abe was busy at the hospital or with his patients but they always had time for each other. She loved him with all of her heart.

"I am sure you will hear something soon, Mother Martha. You did put up a large reward for information and I am sure someone must have seen the two of them by now." She looked at Abe and Zeke for reassurance. They nodded; the two could pass for twins with their blond hair and attractive features.

"All we know for sure is they are heading for Wyoming. Our newfound stepbrother, Jeb Whittaker wants that money and I am sure he won't just forget about it after nearly killing his own flesh and blood over it." Ezekiel could not believe that their biological father, Jebediah Whittaker had another son that none of them knew about, a son with an Indian squaw. Their own stepbrother, who stalked them and almost killed Jeremy. Life had been very interesting since Ezekiel had arrived home from England. Thinking of England reminded him of Abby, he wanted to change the subject. "Oh, by the way, Abby and I are planning to come and spend a few days with you Vivienne, is that alright with you? She misses seeing you and wants to spend some time with you. Abe and I can deal with the hordes of patients that will be lining up outside." He laughed, punching his brother in the shoulder lovingly. Vivienne smiled, she looked forward to Abby's visits.

"Zeke is right, you will hear something soon Mother. You really do need to try and rest. Papa is on the mend, it is just going to take time for his lung to heal but it is healing. His doctor told me that he is very pleased with how he is getting stronger everyday."

"Besides, Nurse Sissy is there, taking care of him. You must hire her to work with you in the clinic, Abe." The brothers did their best to distract Martha and the afternoon was spent in pleasant conversation. Martha seemed much more relaxed on the trip home.

Loretta and Austin were waiting for them when they arrived at the mansion in north St. Louis. "Loretta, Austin, how lovely to see you. How is Jeremy?" She hugged her friends and then excused herself and went straight to her husband's room. He seemed to have more color in his face than earlier that day. "How are you feeling, my Darling?"

"I actually feel a little stronger today, Martha. Nurse Sissy must have fixed me up." He raised his bandaged hand and they both laughed. How she had missed his laughter. She reached over and kissed his hand. "Tomorrow I am going to have Charles set up a place for me in the conservatory. I have been in this room long enough. Time to join the living." She kissed his cheek and smiled her widest smile. He was on the mend. A quiet tap on the door made them both look in that direction.

"Speaking of the living, I was wondering when you were going to join us. I am getting tired of doing all the work." Austin strolled over to the bed, his tall, thin frame moving confidently. He shook his friend's hand, laughing at the sight of the bandages on the other hand. "You look better today."

"I was just saying that I am going to move to the conservatory tomorrow. How are you, Austin?" Martha moved out of the room to give the two friends some time alone. "I must apologize for leaving you in the lurch like this. How are things on the waterfront?" Jeremy was worried about his business as well as his daughter, although he trusted Austin explicitly. He smoothed a wayward lock of hair, now more gray than brown, out of his eyes.

"Everything is fine at the office. I arranged for the cotton to be shipped to England. The furs and pelts left yesterday on their way to Europe and the silk shipment arrived today from the orient. Everything is running smoothly, not that you are not missed, of course. You concentrate on getting better. You will be back in the office in no time. Any word on Anna?"

"Nothing. Austin, I lie here thinking of what could be happening to her with that lunatic. I wonder if Jebediah will ever leave us in peace? The man has been dead for twenty years but still he haunts me." Austin nodded. "I keep thinking about those years long ago when Martha's father sent you and I to find her in the wild Wyoming territory. Now it is as if history is repeating itself, but it is not my brother Jebediah that married Martha and disappeared, but his illegitimate son and Anna. If he is half the bastard that Jebediah was, Anna could be in great danger. I just feel so helpless." Again he pushed the wayward lock of hair out of his eyes. "Ezekiel and Isaac offered to follow them to Wyoming, but what good would that do? She went of her own free will. I am so confused and frustrated." Jeremy was shaken by another coughing spell. Austin looked at his friend with great pity. He too had been wondering just how similar to the senior Jebediah Whittaker, the newfound son was. After all, he stalked the family for months, tried to kidnap Annabelle and Vivienne, leaving them both injured and then showed up at the church demanding the death of Jeremy and the three boys. He was showing all of the signs of being deranged. Anna didn't seem in the least bothered by that fact when she offered to go with him; although it was, or seemed to be, an unselfish act on her part.

"Jeremy, you must concentrate on regaining your strength. I am sure you will hear from Anna soon. Remember when David ran off to join the navy? We were frantic and then one day a letter arrived and it put all of our minds at ease."

Downstairs, Martha stopped to order refreshments from Charles, the butler and then fixed her hair in the mirror in the entrance hall. *Yes, I do look tired. Anna, how can you do this to us?* She went to join Loretta in the great room. Loretta pulled her into her arms, comforting her like no one else could.

"Oh Loretta, if only we would hear from Anna. I know that is what he is waiting for." Loretta nodded, motioning Martha to one of the wingback chairs by the fire. The two women chatted and Martha drew great comfort from Loretta's company. Loretta was careful not to express her opinion of Anna to her friend.

Ezekiel, who had excused himself to the study upon returning, joined the women for brandy. "Mother, that pine in the fireplace smells lovely. It gives the room such a pleasant feel." He inhaled the pungent smell deeply and appreciatively. "Did Abby tell you that we are going out to Abraham and Vivienne's for a few days, Aunt Loretta?" Ezekiel was one of Loretta's favorite people and she could not be more pleased that he and Abby were courting.

"Yes, as a matter of fact she was packing a few things when we left. She told me to tell you she would be ready at 10 tomorrow morning." Martha smiled at the contented look on her son's face. She too was glad of the blooming relationship between their two children.

"Annabelle and the children went back to the farm late this afternoon. Charles tried to convince them to stay but Annabelle was anxious to get home to Isaac. She is such a great help to me. I have been blessed with two wonderful daughter's in law, and possibly a third?" She looked at Ezekiel. He would not meet her gaze and did not reply. Loretta and Martha exchanged a look.

"I have some reading to do, Ladies, if you will excuse me. Tell Abby I will fetch her tomorrow at 10. Good evening, Aunt Loretta, Mother." He turned and left the room. The two women stared after him.

"What was that all about? Is there trouble between Abby and Ezekiel?"

"Not that I know of, and Abby certainly is not showing any signs of losing interest. Perhaps Ezekiel is not as serious as we think. Oh God, Martha, I hope he doesn't break Abby's heart. She has loved him since she was eight years old." Loretta looked worried. Martha patted her hand but did not respond. What could she say? Ezekiel had always been quite the "lady's man" and everyone just assumed he had decided to settle down with Abby. Martha knew he was thinking about England and would have to return there soon. Would he travel alone or ask Abby to go with him as his wife?

Chapter Three

Anna's letter

The train stopped at a small town in Nebraska. Passengers that were continuing on were informed that there would be a two- day layover due to a problem with the tracks.

After a tirade directed at the conductor, Jeb snatched their luggage and stepped onto the train platform. "Two days in this God forsaken hell hole. I want to get to Wyoming." He fumed, grabbing Anna's hand and pulling her along. She pulled her hand away.

"Just relax, you really have to try and control that temper. You are supposed to be a gentleman." Gently she took his arm, smiling coquettishly at him. He exhaled loudly, staring at her, his lips pursed tightly. She nudged him forward much more calmly.

Anna and Jeb walked towards the hotel, observing the western town as they walked. The dwellings were made of rough- cut lumber, some were adobe and salvaged railroad ties were used everywhere. The town consisted of three saloons, two bordellos, a general store and a very unsavory hotel.

The weather was growing colder and Anna pulled her fur cape around her shoulders to ward off the chill. They passed a noisy saloon. "I'm going to go in there for a drink, you go to the hotel and get us a room." Jeb moved off toward the noise.

"Jeb, come back here. I am not walking through this town alone." Several other passengers walked close behind them. Jeb turned to an older woman and her companion.

"Would you mind accompanying my wife to the hotel?" He grabbed Anna's arm and pushed her in the direction of the older woman. The woman nodded and continued walking. Anna sneered at Jeb, rushing to keep up with the others.

"Don't get drunk." Anna shouted after him but she was sure he was out of earshot. She passed the general store, the bordello, and a busy blacksmith shop, trying to absorb the atmosphere and the differences to life in St. Louis. Other than her one trip to New York, Anna Whittaker had led a rather sheltered life in the big city. This was all new and different. She was thrilled. Several men crowded outside the bordello. They shouted and whistled at the passing women. Dust settled on her gown as wagons passed by, although she brushed it away with irritation, the exhilaration of the adventure still surged through her veins. *Better get used to dust, city girl.* She chided herself knowing that Wyoming would not be anything like St. Louis. She was finding new strengths with every passing mile and although she was young, her need to be free and her desire for a challenge were strong.

A man walked in front of the passengers, expelling a large spittle of tobacco. "Riffraff, I don't know how the railroad can expect decent people to stay in a town like this." The older woman from the train was not impressed. "My husband told me that most of these railroad towns were little more than a gathering place for fur traders, outlaws and gold miners. It appears he was right." Anna barely heard the woman, she was absorbing the sights and sounds of the west. Men on the street watched hungrily, as the elegantly dressed women moved toward the hotel.

Later that afternoon, Jeb returned and found her sleeping on the bed. The room was sparsely decorated. A bed, dresser and one chair were the only furniture in the tiny room. The wallpaper was missing in several places and there appeared to be bullet holes above the bed. Jeb wondered how Anna could sleep in such surroundings. *You must adapt more easily than I expected.* He stared at her for a long time. Removing his clothes, he crawled under the covers finding her dressed only in her chemise and pantaloons. She slowly opened her eyes and turned to look at him. “Who invited you into my bed? You smell like a saloon.” She pushed him away. But Jeb was aroused and he would not be deterred. He rolled on top of her and pulled at her pantaloons. She could smell the liquor on his breath. “Get off me.” She pushed at him again but to no avail. “I said, get off.” She shoved him hard and this time he lost the fight and landed with a thud on the floor. He glared at her.

“What did you do that for, you loved it last time.” Too much whiskey had loosened his tongue. He spoke without thinking.

“Last time? What are you talking about? I have never, never been with you. As a matter of fact I have never….” She stopped short of finishing her statement. It was as if a light had gone off in her mind. Of course she must have had sex with someone or how could she explain the miscarriage. She had been with someone in New York but had no recollection of it. She was shocked when she found out she had miscarried. Now she stared at him, vague recollections beginning to form.

He was sobering up quickly. He grabbed for his trousers and started to dress.

She was on him in a flash. She struck him hard across the face. He grabbed her wrist and stared at her face. It was crimson with rage. “You, it was you. You son of a bitch, you raped me and got me pregnant. You knew I was too drunk to know what was happening. You are just lucky I lost the little bastard.” Her whole body was shaking, he pinned her arms down.

“Let’s get something straight. I did not rape you. You wanted it, that’s what you went to New York for. You drank so much you didn’t even care. You loved it, kept telling me not to stop. So don’t you ever say I raped you.” He looked directly into her eyes, “What do you mean you were pregnant?" Her being pregnant had never occurred to him. At the time, she was just a nice bit of entertainment. A lot had happened since then.

"I had a miscarriage and stupid me, didn't remember a thing. I was as shocked as my mother, when I lost it. Good thing too, because a screaming brat is the last thing I want. Now why didn't you tell me it was you, I didn't remember a thing." She was shrieking at him; her fists escaped his grip. She pummeled his chest. He pushed her down on the bed and held her down.

"Calm down and be quiet. That was last summer and a lot has happened since then. I didn't even know you. Just some piece of fluff I met on the train. You tried to seduce me. Don't deny it." He knew that he had followed her to New York and knew exactly who she was but this was not the time to go into details. He wanted to know about the pregnancy. "Now what do you mean you were pregnant."

"What are you stupid? Pregnant. You know, with child?" She was fuming and it would take more than him to calm her down. "You got me pregnant and you won't do it again. Do you hear me? I am going to Wyoming for money, a new life and adventure. I am not going to get pregnant by you or anyone else, ever again. Now go find a saloon girl or go sleep on the floor." She shoved him away and pulled the covers over her. She started to sob. He stood up, watched her for a few minutes and left the room.

He walked the street alone. The night air was cold and crisp. Thousands of stars filled the Nebraska sky, it made him remember how he and his mother would lie on their backs and stare at the wide Wyoming sky when he was young. His mother was Cheyenne; she lived in Fort Laramie and became the unwilling mistress of that horrible man. He beat her and made her do unspeakable things. Red Fox, their son was born and grew to hate the life they had been dealt. His mother told him who his father was, but by the time he was old enough to understand, Jebediah Whittaker, pastor of Whittakerville was dead. His mother died when he was only ten leaving him to fend for himself. His hate for his father, Jebediah Whittaker had kept him alive. When he learned that Jebediah Whittaker had a family, three sons and a wife, he extended his hatred to them. Hate can be a powerful tool when a young boy needs to survive. It was not until last year that he went to Whittakerville and learned that a chest belonging to Jebediah Whittaker had been found. The rest of the family had moved to St. Louis right after the pastor's death. Red Fox, who now called himself Jeb, went to claim the fortune. He remembered how the lawyers had laughed at him, saying that only if the three sons and the brother of Jebediah Whittaker were dead or agreed, would he ever have the right to the inheritance. That is when, blinded by hate for all they had, that he decided to find them. He tracked them to St. Louis and discovered that Martha Whittaker had married Jebediah's brother, Jeremy many years ago. Martha and Jeremy had a daughter, Anna.

He put his plan in motion and spent the summer stalking the family, part of his plan was to exploit young Anna. The thought of Anna turned him back in the direction of the hotel. Anna reminded him of his mother, strong willed, independent and beautiful. Anna was very intelligent and she had led a privileged life. It was a very strange twist of fate that he now found himself traveling back to Whittakerville with a letter giving all of the fortune to him, signed by the rest of the Whittaker men and with the daughter of Jeremy Whittaker by his side. He quickened his pace.

Anna lay staring at the ceiling. She now had many answers to questions that had nagged at the back of her mind for months. She could not remember being with anyone, yet she definitely lost her child. Now she knew, now she could remember bits and pieces of that night in

New York. Jeb was right. She had wanted him. She had wanted to experience what it felt like to be with a man. She went to New York without her parents' permission and drank alcohol for the first time in her young life. She met Jeb on the train and told him she was seventeen. She remembered seeing him in New York but until tonight she had not put it all together. When she returned, her furious parents arranged a betrothal to Hans Kruger. Handsome Hans, she was relieved when she found out it was him. She knew he loved her and she thought she could control him. But Hans proved to be more strong willed than she thought. He claimed to love her but would not do what she asked. He would not buy the mansion she wanted. She did not love him. She did not love anyone. The spur of the moment decision to leave with Jeb was the best decision she had made. She would make up with him. She needed him to get what she wanted. The door opened.

Jeb tiptoed into the darkened room. He sat quietly on the bed. Her hand reached for him. He leaned over her and she pulled him close. His lips pressed to hers. She motioned for him to lay with her. Smiling, she wished him "Good Night." They both turned to face opposite sides of the room and fell fast asleep smiling.

The next morning, Anna wrote a letter to her parents.

Dear Mother and Father:

I am sure that you are worried about me. Please know that I am safe and unharmed. Jeb is not the monster that you think. We will travel to Whittakerville together, where I will again write of my news. Do not follow me. Do not hire anyone to follow me. I want this life, I want to be free and I will be. Father I am relieved to know you are recovering. Jeb did not mean to kill you. It was an accident. Ask the police to stop looking for us.

This is all I have to write for now. Please respect my wishes. If you follow me, I will run away again.
Your daughter,
Anna.

She posted the letter at the Pony Express office before the train left the station. Anna was determined to have the life of her own choosing, a life without rules.

The train moved through the snowy plains of Nebraska. Tiny towns had blossomed on the stark vacant land along the rail lines. Between the towns, lay stretches of vast open plain. Jeb studied under Anna's tutelage growing more confident by the day. She read to him from the newspaper making sure he was absorbing the details of government, railroad acquisitions, and other details that might be used in conversation. Looking up from her paper, she turned to watch the scenery roll past. Lines of wagons could be seen from the window, hundreds of pioneers heading west to make a new life. Although most of the people used the railroad, there were still, a few hardy pioneers that chose to travel by wagon. "My mother and your father traveled on one of those wagon trains to Wyoming. Isn't it strange how fate has brought us together, on the same journey? In much better conditions, of course." Anna could not imagine traveling for months in a wagon. Jeb, who had lived rough on the land, stared out at the wagons. He respected the tenacity of the pioneers. He also understood the impact they would have on the Native Americans that lived and hunted on these lands. Although he had never lived amongst the natives, his mother had told him many stories and taught him some of their customs.

"The Cheyenne and the Lakota won't be very happy to see them." He stared out the window, lost in thought.

Early one morning, Anna read the newspaper as the train moved through the dusty plains. "Listen to this, Wyoming was the first state to grant women the vote. I remember something about that from school. It also says that in Laramie, there was the first all women jury. I am going to like this place. Freedom for women, at last." Jeb just ignored her. She was growing used to his quiet, sullen moods; she continued reading. "Look at this, Wyoming now has electric lights. Looks like this might not be the 'hell hole' I originally thought." He turned to look at her in surprise.

"Hell hole! You had better watch your language, Milady. It appears I am having a bigger influence on you than you are on me." She pursed her lips and made a face at him. Sullenly, he turned back to the window. His dark eyes stared blankly into the passing landscape.

The letter arrived in St. Louis early one morning. Martha was leaving for the Haute Couture when Charles delivered it to her. She stared at the familiar handwriting on the envelope. Shaking, she quickly took it to Jeremy in the great room.

"A letter from Anna." She handed it to him. He was recovering slowly but gaining strength everyday. His hand shook when he held the letter. He opened it slowly, fearing what it would say.

"It appears she is alright," his voice trembled. Martha let the breath she was holding escape, before taking the letter from him. She read the words over and over, and then raised her eyes to her husband. Jeremy stared at her with tears in his eyes. "She wants to be left alone. She wants to go to Wyoming with that man." Martha moved to hold him in her arms. She struggled with her mixed emotions. In her heart she was relieved to know Anna was not harmed but she was angry. Martha could see the hurt in Jeremy's eyes. *Anna you are evil, just like your uncle Jebediah, the man that spawned that horrible man you are with. Good riddance to you.* She shook the thoughts from her mind. Not wanting to upset Jeremy, she thought over what she would say very carefully.

"She does not want us to look for her but she does say she will write from Wyoming. At least she is safe. Are you going to tell the police to stop looking for them?" Jeremy didn't answer. He just nodded his head. The tears rolled down his cheeks; his heart was broken. Martha rocked him in her arms, her tears were for Jeremy, the man she loved with all of her heart, not for her daughter, Anna.

Ezekiel found the two of them, still in their embrace a few minutes later. "What has happened?" He knelt in front of the two forlorn people that he loved. It mattered not that neither one of them were his biological parent, he owed them his life. "What is it? Papa, Mama?" Martha handed him the letter, still clutched tightly in her hand. He stood taking the crumbled paper with him and began to read. "So, they are heading for Wyoming and she does not want us to follow. I guess Loretta and Abby were right; she wanted to go with him. She may have planned the whole thing."

"No, no she would never do that. She is just caught up in the thrill of the adventure." Jeremy was shaken by a coughing spasm. Ezekiel looked at Martha, realizing what he had just said without thinking. Martha stared back. *So, I am not the only one that thought that.*

Ezekiel and Martha calmed Jeremy and left him to rest. The two retired to the conservatory. The windowed room was large and filled to capacity with tropical plants of all sizes and description. Floral scents mingled pleasantly. The light filtered through the windows giving it a soft, romantic feel. "It appears I have let the cat out of the bag, Mama I am so sorry. I never should have said that. It was not my place to repeat what others have said. Abby will be so upset." Martha patted his hand assuredly.

"Loretta and Abby are entitled to their opinion, I have to admit those were my thoughts as well. Please don't tell your Papa. He loves Anna, she is his only child and he refuses to see the evil in that girl."

"Well, I hope that man is enjoying my clothes. It was no coincidence that clothes and money went missing the last time we saw Anna or Jeb. Jr." Martha nodded. She had to agree with him. It didn't look good for Anna. All of the evidence pointed to a well-planned getaway. Ezekiel went to fetch some tea and the two spent the morning, trying to decide how to keep Jeremy from having a setback. Isaac arrived at the mansion.

"Well, what are you two plotting? You both look very serious." He pecked Martha's cheek and took the chair next to his brother. The difference in the brothers' appearance was striking, one blond and the other dark. Isaac's basic uniform consisted of Levi's, a cotton shirt with dark suspenders, cowboy boots and a wide brimmed Stetson. Ezekiel was a stark contrast in ascot tie, white silk shirt, waistcoat and wool trousers. Ezekiel handed him the letter.

"An accident? The rest of you might forgive that bastard for stabbing Papa, but I would like to get my hands on him. He almost killed my wife and he falsely befriended my children, putting them in great danger. That stabbing was no accident, that man is a lunatic." Isaac could not believe that Anna would be so gullible. "I see our little sister is heading for Whittakerville. I hope she has better luck there than we did." A black cloud seemed to appear over his head, his dark eyes stared at the large cactus in front of them, not seeing it. Isaac grew very silent. They knew he was remembering something that happened a long time ago.

"Don't Isaac. Don't even think about that horrible place or that beast. None of us forgive that man; Anna only sees what she wants to see. Help Ezekiel and I decide how to keep Papa from having a setback. I will go and get you some tea." Martha rose and left the two men alone.

"Zeke, I just can't help but think about that day. It has been years but it still haunts us." Isaac stood and began restlessly pacing the room.

"Mama is right, Isaac. Don't think about that or our father; the man was a bastard. He deserved to die. Good luck to Anna and his bastard son, they can have Wyoming, the money and Whittakerville, for all I care. I will never go there again." Zeke put his arm around his brother's shoulder for support. Isaac nodded.

"You're right. It has been more than twenty years and we have good lives here in St. Louis, and you in England. We won't let that man haunt us. Besides, I hate to say this but Anna was nothing but trouble. She can handle herself no matter what Jeb Junior throws her way. In fact, he is the one that should be careful."

"True, look at poor Hans. She chewed him up and spit him out. He is devastated, poor man. For someone so young, she is quite the force to be reckoned with."

"The only good thing about Anna walking out on Hans was that the man has thrown himself into his work. The Haute Couture is doing very well in Mama's absence."

"Thank God, Abby is a gentle, kind and loving woman. You are very lucky to have Annabelle, Isaac." Ezekiel picked a dead flower from the green stem beside his chair.

"I knew I was going to marry Annabelle when I was twelve years old. She is the only woman I have ever wanted. I know you can't say the same, Zeke."

"Well, a man must have variety. That is my theory on women." The two brothers laughed. "Of course, I am getting rather enamored with Miss Wells. Not sure what I'm going to do about that situation."

"Oh, oh. Trouble. I hope you don't intend to break Abby's heart, Zeke. She has loved you since she was a child and I know how that feels. I know you will be returning to England soon. She is a lovely woman and would make a great wife for any man. If you are going to let her down, it better be gently or you will have Mother and Loretta to deal with."

Martha brought the tea. She looked at her two sons, how lucky she was to have raised three fine young men. "What will Loretta and I have to deal with now?"

"Nothing Mama, let's have the tea and then I have to go and see Abby." Zeke gave Isaac a sideways look and the other remained silent. But Isaac was concerned about Zeke's comments. There was enough trouble in this family with Jeremy's recovery and Anna's disappearance. None of them needed another problem to deal with.

Chapter Four

Zeke makes a decision

"Abby, we must talk. Come and sit beside me." Ezekiel motioned to the park bench. The day was sunny and surprisingly warm for this time of year. The two were partaking in a stroll before dinner. They sat opposite the tiny lake, where swans glided gracefully on the calm water. Abby sat beside Zeke and took his hand.

"Why so serious, my Love?" She did not want to think about him leaving for England but was afraid that was what was on his mind.

"Abby, you know I have a wonderful life in England. I must be returning to my teaching position at the boy's school. I was lucky to get the extension for Abraham's wedding but I really must get back." She held her breath in anticipation. Was he about to propose? "England is a very long way from St. Louis. Life there is different." Her eyes showed a sudden sadness, it broke his heart to do this to her. "Abby, you know I am very fond of you but I could never ask you to leave your family."

I would travel to the end of the earth for you my love, please ask me to go with you. She waited silently. He didn't ask her.

"Let's go and have a lovely dinner at the hotel. You and I will enjoy each other's company for another two weeks before I leave for England. Now, no tears, Abby, let me see that beautiful smile." In spite of her heart breaking into a million pieces, Abby smiled at him. She took his arm and walked stoically toward the hotel. Ezekiel walked as if the weight of the world was off his shoulders.

Isaac returned to the farm where his family was waiting. The farm was large and prosperous. It sat on the outskirts of St. Louis. "Pa, Pa did you see the new baby kittens. Silly things having babies at this time of year; cats are dumb." Sissy leaped into his arms. He nuzzled her close then set her down on the ground. Smiling at his wife, he followed Sissy into the barn. Annabelle took the baby into the house; a cool wind was blowing.

Thomas sat at the table completing his homework. "Is Pa home?"

"Yes Thomas, now finish your homework so I can set the table. We will need more wood for the fireplace this evening. After such a lovely day, it is growing cold out there." Annabelle tussled Thomas' dark locks and set Amy into the high chair. Soon the family sat down to dinner, joking and laughing, each sharing their day with the others. Isaac was proud of his family and he would do anything to keep them safe.

"Mama got a letter from Anna today." He picked up a piece of beef and placed it in his mouth. The succulent flavor burst on his tongue. "This is delicious, Annabelle."

"What did the letter say, Isaac?" Annabelle poured more milk for the children, then turned her attention to her husband.

"Apparently, she is going to Whittakerville with that crazy Indian and she says it was just an accident that Papa got stabbed. Accident, my foot!" He quickly remembered the children and continued eating in silence.

"Whittakerville, that is the town that is named after us. Can you tell me about it Pa?" Thomas was dying to know about the town. Last time it was mentioned everyone looked like he had said a bad word. Maybe now he could hear more about it.

"Yes it is, but we will never go there. It was nothing but trouble for us. Now eat your dinner and forget about that place." Thomas put his head down. *What is the big secret about Whittakerville? Auntie Anna is lucky. I bet she won't think it is a bad place.*

"At least we all know she is safe. Anna can handle herself in spite of her age. Now, would anyone like some nice apple pie?" Annabelle rose from the table.

Later that night, Annabelle and Isaac snuggled in their bed. "Do you think Anna had anything to do with that man before the church incident? She seemed to know him."

"I wouldn't put anything past my little sister. I, for one, will not miss her. She gave Mama such grief. Now come here my wife." He reached for her, pulling her into his arms.

"Isaac, don't say that. Family is important no matter what they do. We have to love and accept all of our relatives. I know Anna was troublesome but Jeremy and Martha loved her very much, just as all of you did. She will see sense and come home and when she does, we must forgive her." She looked into his dark eyes and smiled. Isaac was a kind, loving husband and a good father. She knew he didn't mean what he said.

"Forget about Anna, now where were we? I love you Annabelle."

The next morning Isaac rode over to Abe's house to discuss the letter. "I think she was in on it all along, Abe." He set the large milk container down on the porch. Abe thanked him, inviting him in.

"Well, I wouldn't be surprised if she was, but I don't think she would go so far as to have her own father stabbed. I think that was purely his doing. I hope that man is not as bad as our father was. If he is, she has no idea what she is getting herself into." Abe tidied his desk, as the brothers talked. His office was large and held an oak desk, a couple of leather chairs. His medical certificates were proudly displayed over the desk. Several bookcases lined the wall. The waiting room and examination rooms were off to the side. The smell of antiseptic permeated the air. "This is a huge improvement over conditions in Mississippi. I treated the black slaves that had been given their freedom and little else, in nothing more than a shack. You know, Isaac sometimes I miss that life. Those people really needed me."

"You did your best for them Abe, you are a good doctor. People here need you as well. Besides, it is nice having my little brother living so close. Not to mention your wife is the best farm hand I ever had." Isaac picked up the pen on the desk and twirled it in his fingers. "Where is she, by the way?"

"Vivienne went into town to see Abby. Have you spoken to Zeke at all?"

"The other day he said he was not sure what to do about Abby. I hope he doesn't hurt that young woman. She is such a lovely, kind person. Zeke never should have started courting her if he wasn't serious. Now he is talking about going back to England." The pen continued to twirl, around and around. Isaac's tall frame relaxed in the large leather chair.

"Zeke left England to escape one woman, and now he is retreating back there to escape another. I understand the school is waiting for him to return and he loves living in Pheasant Run. I honestly thought he would take her with him as his wife." Abe lifted several files from the desk and put them into the drawer. "Our little brother is quite the lady's man, Isaac. Not like us. One woman our entire lives and I am glad it's that way. Why, I know so little about women, I spent weeks with Vivienne thinking she was a young man." The two brothers laughed remembering how Abe had met Vivienne. Disguised as a boy named Billy, she had fooled him for weeks.

"One woman is enough for me Brother, Amen."

The hotel restaurant was very busy that day. Abby and Vivienne sat beside the windows in the large room. Crisp starched white linen tablecloths and sparkling crystal made the room elegant and welcoming. "I don't believe it. Zeke wouldn't just leave you here."

"That is what he said. He can't ask me to leave my family. Oh, Viv I would go to the end of the earth for that man. I love him so, always have. What am I going to do?" She reached into her bag for her handkerchief. Several men in the restaurant stared in the direction of the two beautiful young women, one blonde, and one brunette.

"There, there, Abby don't cry. He hasn't left yet. He might change his mind. Why don't you just ask him to take you with him?" Vivienne was raised in Louisiana and saw nothing improper about speaking her mind.

"Oh dear God, I could never do that. I must wait until he asks me. It looks like he will just leave me here without a thought, how could I be so wrong. I was sure he loved me." She dabbed her eyes. Just then a handsome young man with dark hair stopped at their table.

"Miss Wells, Mrs. Whittaker, how lovely to see you this afternoon. I trust all is well with you both?" He tipped his hat and continued toward his table.

"Now there is a great catch for someone, Hans Kruger, Anna's castoff. Why she would throw him over is beyond me. He is very handsome." Vivienne's eyes followed Hans.

"Vivienne, you are a married woman! But you are right, he is very handsome." She giggled and Vivienne joined her. The tension was broken at last. The two young women enjoyed their lunch. As they rose to leave the restaurant, Hans Kruger stared appreciatively at Abby. *Perhaps it is time to move on, my broken heart must heal sometime. Yes, it is time for me to ask a certain young lady to dinner.* Hans finished his lunch, paid the check and with a lighter step, returned to his office at the St. Louis Haute Couture.

Later, Vivienne and Abby stopped by the dress shop to visit Martha and Loretta. They were surprised to find Hans alone. Vivienne poked Abby in the ribs, gesturing toward the young man. "Go and speak to Hans, he is staring at you. I think he is interested," Viv teased. A shy Abby asked Hans if her mother and Martha would be back soon.

"No, Miss Wells, they have gone to see one of the suppliers." He realized his hands were sweating nervously. "Miss Wells, I wonder if I could have the pleasure of your company tomorrow evening. The symphony starts at 7." He stared at the floor shyly waiting for a response. Abby was taken aback. She was heartbroken over Ezekiel and the last thing she wanted to do was go out with someone else.

"She would love to, wouldn't you Abby?" Vivienne stepped in to rescue the situation. Abby glared at her. Impeccable manners and years of training overtook her anger and she graciously accepted the invitation.

"I would be honored, Mr. Kruger. I will see you at 7." He beamed with delight, took her hand, gently placing a kiss on it. Abby blushed, Vivienne smiled widely. She took Abby's arm and ushered her out the door before she could change her mind.

"What on earth did you do that for? You knew I couldn't refuse. Vivienne, I am very angry with you." Abby turned on her heel haughtily and started down the street. Vivienne followed, catching up to her easily.

"Oh, for Heaven's sake. Don't you see? If you go out with Hans, Zeke will get jealous. You are too innocent for your own good. Now, listen to me." Vivienne took her arm and soon had Abby's complete attention.

Vivienne returned home to find Isaac with Abe. She poured herself a coffee and joined the two men at the table. "Did you two know that Zeke is going back to England without Abby?"

"I can never get used to seeing you in a dress, Viv," Isaac joked. Abe laughed, staring appreciatively at his wife. The pale yellow dress accentuated her dark hair and slim body. The overskirt added curve to her slim hips and the bodice revealed just a hint of bosom. Abe smiled.

"We were talking about it earlier. All we can do is wait and see what happens. I think Abby is going to need you to help pick up the pieces, Viv." Isaac picked up his cup and sipped the hot black liquid.

"Oh, maybe not." Vivienne gave Abe an impish smile.

"I've seen that look before. What did you do now, Vivienne?" Abe knew his wife very well. Isaac was enjoying the interaction between the two of them.

"Hans Kruger is taking Abby to the symphony tomorrow night."

"What! How on earth did that happen? Oh, I see. You had something to do with it, didn't you?" Abe looked at her, waiting for an answer. Isaac laughed. He had always liked Vivienne's openness and casual southern attitude.

"Don't worry about the details, just make sure that Zeke goes to the symphony with you tomorrow night. I will say I am not feeling well and you can take him instead. Now stop looking at me like that, this will work. Trust me." She drained her cup and left the kitchen. The two men stared at each other and then burst into fits of laughter.

"Zeke, the lady's man has met his match!" Isaac roared slapping Abe on the back.

The next night, Abe and Zeke arrived at the symphony sharply at seven. Several women watched the two blond, handsome young men in formal dress, with interest. The men made their way to their seats in the balcony. The ladies were dressed in their finest attire. The scent of perfume filled the hall. The young men stretched their long frames in the comfortable velvet chairs. Periodically the trill sound of a flute or clarinet could be heard from the orchestra pit, as the musicians took their places.

Abby and Hans arrived minutes later and sat on the main floor just to the left and below the Whittakers' private balcony. Abby took special care with her appearance. Her gown was a rich shade of rose, her blonde hair piled high on her head, two ringlets fell gently at her temples. Long white gloves covered most of her arms. She was stunning. Hans was bewitched. They chatted about the symphony and their favorite classical pieces. She was surprised at how suave and sophisticated he was. She was enjoying herself in spite of her reservations about this entire evening.

The conductor tapped his baton, opening with Mozart's 40th. Zeke looked at Abe in surprise, "I am surprised the conductor would start with this piece. Did you know the 40th Symphony is sometimes referred to as the "Great" G minor symphony, to distinguish it from the "Little" number 25 G minor symphony? Mozart only wrote 2 minor symphonys." Abe nodded, enjoying the music.

Zeke looked over the audience as the music began. His face suddenly went pale. Abe watched him out of the corner of his eye. "What is the matter Zeke? You look ill."

Zeke stared silently at Abby and Hans. She was smiling, how beautiful she looked. He stood up. "I will be back in a minute." Abe grabbed his arm.

"Sit down and tell me what's wrong." Zeke motioned toward Abby and Hans. Abe took a deep breath and then looked at his brother.

"You told her that you were going back to England. You did not ask her to go with you as your wife, so what did you expect?" He waited for the anger on Zeke's face to subside. It was obvious that he was furious. "You can't have it both ways, Zeke. If you don't want her, someone else will. She is beautiful, intelligent and loving. She won't wait around for you forever." Abraham felt sorry for Zeke but it was his own fault.

"Forever! Looks like she didn't wait five minutes. I'm leaving." With that he stood and marched from the balcony. Taking the stairs two at a time, Abe followed his brother from the Music Hall. Zeke would not speak to Abe during the carriage ride back to the mansion. He went directly to his room when they arrived. Abe found Martha and Jeremy in the great room.

"Where is your brother? Why are you back so soon?" Martha looked curiously at Abraham. He shrugged.

"How are you this evening, Papa?" Jeremy smiled and motioned toward the chess game. "Sure, I will beat you at chess before I leave. Ask Charles to bring me a brandy, please Mama." Abraham and Jeremy settled down to play chess and Martha, puzzled, left them alone.

Upstairs, Ezekiel paced back and forth in his room. He ran his hand through his thick blond locks; his entire body was tense. *How could she? With the man that was to marry my sister, that is too much. Abby, oh my Abby what have I done?* His mind and his heart were in turmoil. He didn't want to leave her, he didn't want a wife, and he didn't want her to marry someone else. What did he want? He paced for hours.

Hans delivered Abby to her front door, kissed her hand and thanked her for a lovely evening. She smiled, opening the door and stepping in. Loretta was waiting for her. "How was your evening?" Loretta was quite the matchmaker herself and in fact was responsible for Jeremy and Martha's wedding. She was intrigued with Vivienne's idea to make Ezekiel jealous. Abby was smiling.

"My evening was very nice. I think Zeke saw us but I can't be sure. I noticed he was not in the balcony after the first set. Hans is a very good companion. He loves the opera and has asked me to accompany him next week." Loretta watched her daughter closely. Was it possible she was interested in Hans? Had Ezekiel just been a girlish crush? "Mother, don't look at me like that. I like Hans but I love Zeke. I don't know if this plan of Viv's is a good idea or not. Time will tell." She hugged her mother and went to bed. That night she dreamt of dancing with Zeke under the stars. The evening was warm and the scent of magnolias filled the air.

Chapter Five

Wyoming

"Anna, wake up. We are in Wyoming." Jeb looked out the window at the familiar scenery. She rolled sleepily from her bunk and joined him at the window.

"So this is our new home. It better be nicer than the town we stopped in." She turned and kissed him on the lips. He pulled her to him. She responded, and then pushed him away. "Oh, no you don't. I told you, no brats for me." She started to get dressed. Frustrated, he went back to the window and sat silent and sullen for the next hour. Anna went to the dining car for breakfast.

"Next stop, Fort Laramie." The conductor made his way through the cars. People started to show their excitement at reaching their destination. Anna was tingling with anticipation. *What will it be like? How long before we get the money? Where will we live?* She spent the next hour planning her future.

Jeb was dressed when she returned to the sleeper. He was angry. "I don't know why I brought you here in the first place. You are driving me insane." He glared at her.

"Calm down. What do you want from me? I taught you to read a little, you can sign your name, you have a new identity and you are home. So get over it. Now let's pack up and be ready to get off in Whittakerville." She reached for her clothes and placed them carefully into the bag. He wanted to slap her. He grabbed her and spun her around. He pressed his lips to hers firmly. She tried to pull away but he held her tight. She felt his lips pressing hers and his tongue struggling to enter her closed mouth. She wanted him to stop but felt herself responding. Her lips parted just enough to encourage him. He threw her down on the bunk. Her skirt was up over her head and he was pulling at her pantaloons. She kicked at him. Her foot caught him squarely on the jaw. In pain, he struck out and hit her across the face. She kicked again wildly, her fingernails dug into his arm. Again he hit her. She rolled off the bunk, he followed and pinned her to the floor. "You pig, you are just like your evil father. You are nothing but a filthy rapist." At the mention of his father, his grip loosened. His hands dropped to his side and he stared at her. The blank look frightened her more than the attack. "Get off me, you pig." She shoved him roughly. He fell away from her. She took advantage of the moment and jumped to her feet, grabbing the mirror from the bag, she held it over her head. "Come near me again and I will sink this mirror into your skull. Now get out." He crawled toward the door. Opening it as he rose, without looking at her, he left her alone. Anna sunk down onto the bunk. Heavy sobs wracked her body. She lifted the mirror to see the cut on her cheek. *What have I gotten myself into? I won't be able to fight him off forever.* She tended to her cut and finished packing her bags.

Jeb stood at the back of the caboose watching the landscape disappear. *Am I just like you? I hate you Jebediah Whittaker, no I won't be like you. I won't.* He straightened his clothing and turned back to the sleeper cabin. She opened the door just as he was about to knock. "So you're back. Well, pack your bags and let's get off this God forsaken train for once and for all. I have had quite enough of train travel." He stared blankly. "Hurry up. What are you waiting for? We have a fortune to claim." With that he pushed past her and shoved his belongings into his bag.

"Anna." She turned toward him. "I'm sorry. I'm not like him. I'm not." She walked away without responding.

After departing the train, the travelers took a wagon the last mile to Whittakerville Hotel. Anna was impressed with the beauty of the landscape. Jeb was broody and silent.

He had waited almost a year for this moment. Finally he would have money and power. He could taste it. Anna could see that this town was much older and more developed than most of the train stops along the way. She was relieved to see the hotel was a newer building and the rooms presentable. They checked into the hotel and went directly to the lawyer's office.

Whitehall and Johnson, Attorneys at Law, the two young people stared at the sign. Taking a great breath of air, squaring their shoulders and squeezing each other's hand, they opened the door. A pert receptionist greeted them. "May I help you?" She didn't recognize Jeb from his previous visit almost a year ago.

"Yes, my husband is Jeb Whittaker and we are here to see Mr. Whitehall." Anna took charge.

"One moment please. Have a seat." The young woman moved toward one of the offices. Jeb sat in one of the chairs, his back straight and tense. Anna remained standing.

"Mr. Whitehall will see you now." The two young people entered the huge, wood paneled office. A tall, white haired man was standing behind a large mahogany desk.

"Mr. And Mrs. Whittaker? What can I do for you?" He extended his hand; Jeb ignored it. Anna reached forward and shook his hand, a very unorthodox move for a woman. He smiled at her. "Please have a seat." Anna took the chair directly in front of the desk, Jeb wandered around the room nervously, his bowler hat clutched firmly in his hand.

"My husband is Jeb Whittaker, I believe you have an inheritance here for him. An inheritance from his father, Pastor Jebediah Whittaker?"

"If I remember correctly, there are other relatives that may have a claim to that money. Let me get my files." He walked slowly from the room staring at Jeb as if he was trying to remember him.

"See, he doesn't recognize you. That is good. Now sit down for heaven's sake. You are making me nervous." Reluctantly, he took the chair next to hers.

"Yes, I was correct, there may be some other relatives with a claim. I am afraid I can't help you." Whitehall took his seat behind the desk as if to dismiss them. Jeb leapt toward the man, about to grab his lapels. Mr. Whitehall turned white, a loud gasp rose in his throat. Anna pulled Jeb back; he was fuming. Quickly, trying to regain some control Anna produced the letter.

"I believe this is what you need. Jeb, please let the man read the letter." She gave him a very stern sideways glance. Jeb glared at Whitehall. Jeb's face was crimson with rage and he was close to losing control. The other man watched him nervously as he took the paper from Anna's outstretched hand. "Now, our money if you please." Mr. Whitehall read the letter.

We, Jeremy Whittaker brother of Jebediah Whittaker and his sons, Isaac, Abraham and Ezekiel hereby declare that all and any monies and or property located or discovered in Whittakerville belonging to Jebediah Whittaker be given to his son, Jeb Whittaker. We identify the bearer of this note to be the son of Jebediah Whittaker. We revoke any and all claim to said monies. We sign this decree this day in St. Louis.

The letter was signed by all of the Whittaker men. He looked up defiantly at the two young people in front of him. "I don't think this will be enough. I am afraid you will have to leave now. You stay away from me, Mr. Whittaker." Jeb started to rise from the chair. Anna put her hand on his arm, signaling him to sit down.

"Oh, I don't think so, Mr. Whitehall. My uncle is William Hale, Governor of Wyoming territory. I don't think he will be very impressed by your attitude or your poor treatment of his favorite niece." Anna fluttered her eyelashes confidently, as Mr. Whitehall turned pale. Jeb just stared at Anna in confusion. What was she talking about?

"Shall we go and send a telegram to dearest Uncle Willy, Jeb? This man doesn't seem to want to be very cooperative." She rose and signaled Jeb to do the same.

"Wait. Perhaps I have been a little hasty. Let me see that letter again." Mr. Whitehall was frightened of Jeb but the mere mention of William Hale turned him to ice. Anna pushed it toward him. "Oh yes, of course. This is fine. Come back tomorrow and I will have all the paperwork ready." He forced a smile at Jeb and Anna, both staring at him coldly.

"I don't think so, Mr. Whitehall. Now go and get the money and the paperwork. We don't have time to come back tomorrow. Jeb, why don't you go and send that telegram and I will wait here for the money?" Jeb looked at her confused. Mr. Whitehall exited quickly. Jeb whispered to Anna.

"What the hell are you doing? That Hale guy is not your uncle."

"Shh, just keep quiet and watch. You have a lot to learn. Now fix your cravat, you are about to become a very wealthy man. And keep that temper in check."

After about ten minutes, Mr. Whitehall appeared carrying a large satchel. He placed it on the desk and opened it. Anna suppressed a gasp. The bag contained gold bars, jewelry, money, and several official documents. She removed one of the papers and realized it was a deed. Jeb reached in and took a gold bar from the bag.

"How do I know this is all there was? Maybe you helped yourself before you brought it in here?" Jeb glared at the man making him very nervous. This one was dangerous, Mr. Whitehall could tell by the look in his eyes. Sweat formed on his brow.

"Of course, this is all there is. I assure you, sir. I am a lawyer not a thief."

"Don't worry, Jeb Honey. If we find out that Mr. Whitehall removed anything from this satchel, Uncle Willy will take care of it. You know how he hates vermin."

"Please sign here, Mr. Whittaker and you may take your money. It has been my pleasure." He held the pen out to Jeb. Jeb glanced sideways at Anna. Anna picked up the paper and read it.

"Go ahead and sign it, Jeb." She placed it in front of him. He pretended to read it and signed his name. "The pleasure is all ours, Mr. Whitehall."

"Please give my regards to your uncle, Mrs. Whittaker." Mr. Whitehall showed them to the door, happy to see the back of the pair of them. He had been hoping no one would claim the satchel and had already taken several gold bars for himself. Now he hoped it would not come back to haunt him. "Good day."

Anna and Jeb took the bag and headed for the hotel. They dumped the contents out on the bed and stared at it in disbelief. "Wow, when you said a bag of treasure, I had no idea. These deeds must be worth a fortune. It looks like you own half of Whittakerville." She turned and gave him a huge hug. He was smiling for the first time in a long time. He hugged her gently; the memory of what had happened on the train was haunting him.

"I wouldn't have it, if it weren't for you Anna, you were so amazing in that lawyer's office. I would have beaten him to a pulp. What made you think of the Uncle Willy thing?" She saw a new respect in his eyes and she liked it.

"I read about him in the paper, apparently he is a real mean so and so. Most of the court officials are afraid of him so I thought I would try it. It worked, Jeb. Look at all this loot." She picked up a necklace that seemed to be emeralds and rubies. "Put this on me, I want to see how I look." Like a pair of children, they played with the jewels, admired the gold bars and threw the money in the air. Jeb was truly happy for the first time in his life. After a few minutes Anna looked at Jeb, smiling. She was pleased with him and with herself.

"I was proud of you today, Jeb. You handled yourself very well in that office. Except for that one little slip, you acted the perfect gentleman." He beamed under her praise. "I want you to know that I forgive you for what happened on the train. Let's just forget it ever happened." She put her arms around his neck and kissed him gently. He kissed her back. He stared into her green eyes, losing his heart. Anna led him to the bed and sat down motioning for him to sit beside her. "We can't have intercourse Jeb, because I don't want to get pregnant. I do care for you. I really do."

"But I can give you a drink that will prevent it, Anna. My mother taught me many of the Indian customs. There is a plant that grows wild here and when women drink the tea, they do not get pregnant. I can get you some if you want." He was taking a chance but he wanted her desperately. She was looking at him with skepticism.

"Are you sure this will work?"

"Absolutely, all the Indian squaws use it. They don't tell the men but I know my mother said it works. Can we try it?" He looked at her excitedly. "I will go and pick some right now." He reached up and gently stroked her bruised cheek. "I am sorry."

"Slow down, boy. I might try it but we don't have to rush. We have more important things to do. Now let's take a walk and find all of these properties. Mr. Landowner." She giggled and grabbed his hand. He went willingly, still thinking about finding those plants and taking her to bed. Anna was thinking about money, lots of money.

Whittakerville was a thriving pioneer town. Anna and Jeb strolled down the dusty street passed the tinsmith and wheelwright shop, the barbershop, the post office and the saloon. There were two banks, a clothing store, a Chinese laundry and sawmill. At the saddlery, Jeb stopped and bought a large Stetson hat. "This is more like it, we are not in St. Louis anymore, Anna." Although he agreed with her new wardrobe choices, he was not comfortable with the small- rimmed bowler hats. He admired himself in the dirty glass of the next shop, "Much better."

The town was larger than Anna had anticipated. Anna stopped to browse in the dress shop but came out empty handed. "Nothing that suits, Milady?" Jeb inquired.

"You must be joking, ready-to-wear is not for me. I have enough dresses for a short while and they have a catalogue in there for made to measure. I guess it is true what they say about pioneer woman having to suffer. Ready-to-wear, indeed." Jeb just rolled his eyes.

Many small cottages sprouted around the perimeter of the town, side streets extended off the main street, some with houses, others filled with small shops. They found the blacksmith shop and walked right in. A burly man covered in black soot and sweat, barely acknowledged them. He pounded a glowing horseshoe with his hammer.

"Excuse me, sir. We are looking for the owner." Anna brushed a spark from her sleeve. Her nosed wrinkled at the smell of perspiration and burning metal. The man stopped what he was doing.

"Who wants to see him?"

"Your landlord, Jeb Whittaker, that's who." The man looked confused.

"Old Jebediah Whittaker has been dead for twenty years. Not likely he is looking for me." He picked up his tools in a large, knurled hand, laughing, about to continue what he was doing.

“This is Jeb Whittaker, his son and the owner of this property. We want to talk to you about your rent.” The man stopped in his tracks and stared open mouthed at the pair.

“My rent? You got a deed?”

“First, let us introduce ourselves. I am Anna Whittaker and this is Jeb Whittaker. You are?” She waited, poised and polished for his answer.

“Smithers, Bill Smithers. I bin the blacksmith in these here parts for more than two decades. Didn’t know the parson had any sons other than the three that left here after he died. You ain’t one of them boys. I remember them.”

Jeb spoke for the first time since entering the building. Remembering Anna’s earlier praise, he stretched out his hand to the man. “Jeb Whittaker at your service, sir. I hope we can reach an agreement.” He shook the man’s filthy hand and Anna was very surprised but impressed. Smithers seemed more comfortable talking to a man. Jeb produced the deed to the blacksmith shop.

“Yep, looks like you own it alright. How much rent you want. I ain’t paid none for years but I run a good business here and I believe in paying what’s due. Ask anyone.”

“I think five dollars a month will be sufficient. Is that a fair amount?” Jeb was really starting to get into this role. “You can consider all of the time before this as a gift.”

“Five it is, here is the first payment. Real nice meeting you, how long you staying?” Jeb took the five dollars and put it in his pocket, his first payment as a landowner. He was going to like this life. Anna nodded to him and moved out of the shop leaving Jeb to conclude the conversation.

“Staying in town, wife and I are looking for a nice house. Thank you, Mr. Smithers and keep up the good work.” He tipped his hat and followed Anna into the street. The blacksmith picked up his hammer and went back to work. *Nice couple, rather uppity for this part of the country but they might fit in.*

Out in the street the two young people could hardly believe how easy this was. They were both intoxicated with power and excitement. "May I buy you dinner, Mrs. Whittaker? Now that I am a wealthy landowner, I can afford the finest roast beef in town. This way, Milady." He laughed, extended his arm like a fine gentleman would, and walked her towards the hotel. Anna walked along the street wondering just how many of the other buildings he owned. She had many thoughts running through her head. *Just remember, the deeds are his, not yours, keep him happy.* Unconsciously she reached for her cheek. The bruise was disappearing but the memory was still vivid. *I will have to watch myself with Jeb. But, I can handle him. At last, I am free.*

Over the next few weeks, Anna and Jeb contacted and collected rent from five more tenants including the boarding house, the feed mill and three houses. Another of the houses that Jeb held the deed for was empty. It was a very large house but in need of repair. "Let's get a crew in here and have it fixed up. It could be a very nice house and it is the biggest in the town. Just think how everyone would look up to you, Jeb. The biggest house in town and the owner of several properties." Anna was very convincing. Jeb liked the sound of that. The old place appealed to him. It was a two story with a widow's walk on top of the roof. A large porch surrounded the entire house.

Jeb soon hired a crew and the repairs began. In the meantime, he and Anna stayed in the hotel. One day they visited the churchyard where Jebediah Whittaker was buried. An old woman approached them.

"Did you know the good Pastor Whittaker? Of course, you both look too young." They looked at the rotund old woman with disinterest. "I asked if you knew him or knew his family?"

"I am his son." The surprised, old lady studied his face.

"Which one, you don't look familiar and I knew the family."

"I am the youngest, Jeb. Who might you be?" The old woman looked at him suspiciously.

"You do look a might like the Pastor Whittaker, same dark hair and eyes. Nice to meet you, I am Olga Mueller; I knew Martha and the boys very well. Were you born after she left Whittakerville?"

"Nice to meet you, Mrs. Mueller." Jeb was wondering if the old woman would make a connection to Anna. Anna took the extended wrinkled hand but did not give her relationship to Martha away. Jeb took the lead. "My wife, Anna and I are settling in this town. We are fixing up the old Hansen house." Olga Mueller looked confused but didn't say anything untoward. She nodded and then moved off. Jeb was getting to be a very smooth talker.

"Weird old bat." Anna watched her go. "She doesn't look like she remembers what day it is, never mind who is who." Anna looked at Jebediah Whittaker's grave, tossed her hair and walked away. Jeb walked over, spat on the grave and joined her. "Old busy body will tell everyone in town what you just told her, maybe you should have kept it to yourself."

"I have to tell people something. They need to know I am Jebediah's son, especially since I have his name and his land holdings. Stop picking on the old lady, she seemed harmless to me. I assume you don't want anyone to know you are Martha Whittaker's daughter, so we will stick with the 'wife' story for now."

"No, I don't. I don't need anyone writing a letter to my parents in St. Louis. I am enjoying the freedom. Besides, I like the façade of man and wife. Yes, let's go and see the house. I am so excited about moving in."

The renovations were almost complete. All of the outer surfaces had been painted and repaired, with new doors and windows installed. The inside was repainted. A week before, Anna had shrieked at the painter, when the color was not the shade she wanted. Jeb was surprised at the rage she displayed over painting a room. She screamed and waved her fists at the poor man, her actions almost hysterical. Jeb knew she wanted the house to be perfect but he didn't think her actions were justified. However desiring peace, he stayed out of it. The poor man was terrified and promised to repaint immediately. Anna was satisfied now. New floors were installed and only the kitchen remained in need of repair. The two walked through the house. "Won't be long we will have a nice kitchen, where you can cook us some delicious fancy dinners." Jeb was growing very fond of this house already. It was spring; he could imagine roses blooming in the garden.

"Ha, that will be the day. You mean the cook will cook us some fancy dinners. These hands do not cook or clean, so get that through your head. We will need at least three servants." Jeb looked at her, no point in arguing. They continued up the large circular staircase. "I will have to have this banister fixed, I don't like the stain." Jeb just rolled his eyes at her. Anna seemed to be obsessed with the house. "This bedroom is lovely. Look at the view of the hills in the distance. Wyoming really is a lovely place. The grasses are like gold, and you know how I love gold." She laughed and he put his arms around her.

"Three servants for Milady, it shall be. Now did you drink your tea this morning?" He had been successful in talking her into drinking the tea but so far they had not had sex. He waited patiently for her to answer him, staring at the golden grasses of Wyoming.

"Yes, I did. How long did you say I should drink it before it will work?" She was actually anxious to have a physical relationship with him. It would give her another hold over him that would keep him with her, him and his money.

"At least seven days, it has been nine. But who's counting." The two of them laughed out loud.

That night, she let him come to her. He was anxious but kept repeating over and over in his head, *I am not like him. I am not like him.* Jeb was very gentle with her. She was surprised. Not remembering much of their first sexual encounter, her curiosity for the experience was overwhelming. She urged him on. He was falling in love with her. He wanted her to love him. She wanted sex. When they were both satisfied, he put his arms around her. She snuggled, content in his arms. *So that is what the older girls meant by unbelievable.* She was truly a woman now. Jeb was sleeping but Anna lay awake planning the move into the new house, the hiring of the servants and how to become the most prestigious woman in Whittakerville.

Chapter Six

On the Farm

Vivienne sat in the kitchen of Isaac and Annabelle's farmhouse. Annabelle was seated on a small stool in the corner. In front of her was a plunger type butter churn. She moved the handle up and down. The sound of the handle blended rhythmically into the background as Vivienne talked. Sissy and Thomas were seated at the table listening to tales of the south. Vivienne was a wonderful storyteller. "In Mississippi, the rivers flow into the delta. One is called the 'Singing River.' On certain days when the wind blows just the right way, you can hear the river singing. My Pa and I heard it many times."

"River's can't sing. They're made of water." Sissy was skeptical, but she loved Viv's stories. Thomas waited patiently for Vivienne to continue.

"Yes, it does sing, Sissy. When the wind blows through the Sawgrass you can hear a sound like wailing. Once a long time ago, a tribe of Indians named the Pascagoula lived there. They were gentle, contented people. The Biloxi Indians also lived there and they were enemies of the Pascagoula."

"Oh, did they have a war?" Sissy, at six had little patience.

"Anola, princess of the Biloxi tribe, was in love with Altama, Chief of the Pascagoula tribe. She was betrothed to a chieftain of the Biloxi, but she ran away with Altama to his people. This Biloxi chieftain led his Biloxi braves to war against Altama and the peace loving Pascagoula. The Pascagoula swore they would either save the young chieftain and his bride or perish with them. When the battle started, the Pascagoula were outnumbered. They were faced with enslavement by the Biloxi tribe or death. The women and children led the way, Pascagoula, accompanied by the princess and Chief Altama, joined hands and began to chant a song of death. They walked into the river until the last voice was hushed by the dark, engulfing waters." Vivienne took a sip of her tea, watching the faces of the children.

"Oh, no, they all drown. That is a sad story, Auntie Viv." Sissy was overcome with sadness. She gave Vivienne a big hug.

"Yes, Sissy and that is who you can hear singing in the Singing River to this day. The sound is very sad and mournful. Now, shall we go and feed those ducks?" Vivienne cleared the dishes, smiling at Annabelle. She headed for the door, followed by Sissy and Thomas.

"Don't forget to come and get some of this butter before you go home." Annabelle rubbed her shoulders before continuing the arduous task. Thomas looked at his mother.

"Should I take over now, Mama?" Thomas inquired, hoping she would say no.

"You go and help with the barn work, I can manage." Thomas turned toward Vivienne.

"Thanks Aunt Viv, I love your stories. I would like to go to Mississippi one day and hear the Singing River." Thomas picked up his hat, holding the door for the two females. He waited until the door was closed before adding, "I would like to go to Wyoming too, but I don't think that is likely." Thomas kicked a stone across the yard. "Aunt Anna is lucky," he added as an afterthought, which did not go unnoticed by Vivienne.

Later that day, she mentioned it to Isaac. Isaac pitched the manure from the stalls while Vivienne groomed the horses. "Thomas won't let Whittakerville go, Isaac, you are going to have to tell him something. He is a young boy, with a town named after his family, that no one will talk about." She ran her hand down the horse's muscled back.

"I know Viv, but we don't want to think about those days. He will just have to forget it." Isaac knew it was unlikely his son would forget, but he would not discuss Whittakerville with anyone. The memories were too painful. After the chores, knowing she had made no progress with Isaac, Vivienne tried reasoning with Annabelle.

"Annabelle, you have to give Thomas some information. He is not letting this go. I asked Isaac to talk to him but he refused. Someone has to tell Thomas why no one wants to talk about that place." Annabelle nodded but remained silent. She stacked the split wood in the wood stove. "I know I am new to this family but children should not be kept in the dark. It will only lead to danger, look what happened with Red Fox." The mention of the man's name made shivers go down Annabelle's spine. "That man almost killed both of us, yet he sat calmly and casually with Thomas and Sissy, befriending them. Now, I want you to seriously think about talking to your children." Annabelle knew that Vivienne was right but she also had to respect Isaac's wishes.

"Vivienne, you are right. Can you perhaps ask Mother Martha to talk to them?"

"Mother Martha? Why can't you do it?" Vivienne was getting agitated. What was the big secret that kept this family silent? Vivienne watched as Annabelle replaced the top on the stove. She went to the pump and washed her hands, blackened from the soot. Drying them on her apron, she took the seat opposite Vivienne.

"Isaac is the head of this house and I must respect his wishes. Please Vivienne, I know you want the best for this family and I do agree that the children need some information. Mother Martha is the only one that might be able to shed some light on this situation without telling them too much. If you ask her, I can stay out of it. You can tell her we discussed it. I will leave it up to you."

Annabelle walked Vivienne to her horse, she waved goodbye and watched until Vivienne was out of sight. A hot wind blew across the farmyard. *Summer is coming, good luck to Anna in a hot, dry Wyoming summer.*

Vivienne rode into the yard of her home, stabled her horse and went to find Abe. He was just finishing some paperwork in his office. "How was the farm? You go take a hot bath and I will be in shortly." He kissed her cheek, returning to his work. Vivienne decided to take his advice, have her bath, cook supper and then talk to him. She heated the water on the stove, lost in thought. She set the freshly churned butter on the counter, licking her finger, when some escaped the bowl. She relished the rich, creamy taste.

Soon she had the tub filled with warm water. She let her body feel the relaxing heat. Vivienne's body was muscled and lean. She was not afraid of physical work and a hot bath was one way that she could relax. Her body relaxed but her mind was reeling. *I am going to get to the bottom of this.*

Abraham helped Vivienne empty the tub. "The plumbers will be here next week to install the indoor plumbing. I know it will be a luxury that you will enjoy, my love."

"I was raised on washtubs and outhouses, Abe. It really doesn't bother me that much."

"As a doctor, I would not have recommended indoor plumbing until a few years ago. When George Waring discovered that plumbing should be vented, he saved many lives. Did you know that people were getting sick from the fumes from their indoor plumbing? The plumbing was venting back into the houses. We doctors were mystified to find out the cause of so much illness. That all changed with Mr. Waring's book, The Sanitary Drainage of Homes and Towns." Abraham looked at

Vivienne. "The look on your face tells me I am boring you. But, I guarantee you will be happy when you don't have to go outside in the middle of winter." He laughed.

There was something else on Vivienne's mind as she hung the tub on the wall in the back room.

Over coffee, she broached the taboo subject. "I asked Isaac and Annabelle to talk to Thomas about Whittakerville." Abe gave her a startled look.

"Why did you do that? You know we don't discuss it. I wish you would just leave it alone, Viv. Those days are not worth remembering. That place holds nothing but nightmares for all of us." Vivienne looked at her husband. *What on earth happened to all of you in Wyoming? Thomas isn't the only one that wants to know. I need to know too.*

"Can you please tell me what happened, Abe? I am your wife, I want to share your past and your pain." She held his hand in hers, looking into is haunted eyes.

"Just leave it Vivienne. Now, pass the coffee please. Tell me about Abby. Has Ezekiel made any sign of changing his plans to return to England?" Vivienne knew better than to insist, she would ride into St. Louis and speak with Martha tomorrow. One way or another, she was going to find out exactly what the big secret was.

Martha was surprised to see Vivienne in the great room with Jeremy. "Vivienne my dear, what a lovely surprise. Did you come to town with Abraham?" Martha kissed Viv's cheek and then sat with her husband.

"Abe dropped me off on his way to the hospital. I wondered if I might have a word in private with you, Mother Martha?" Jeremy and Martha exchanged a look.

"Of course, my dear, let's go into the conservatory shall we? The weather is cool today but that room is always bright and sunny. The doctor is coming to see Jeremy so we shall leave him here."

"Lovely to see you again, Vivienne. Thomas was telling me that you would have him ready for the fair. He is very excited." Jeremy pulled the blanket over his knees, as a chill ran through him.

"Thomas will win the riding competition, for sure. He is very good at jumping and Chestnut trains easily. You take care of yourself, Papa Jeremy." Martha and Vivienne moved into the hall towards the conservatory.

"You are very kind to speak with me, Mother Martha. I am afraid I might upset you but I have some questions that need answering." Martha looked at the young woman, wondering what this was about. After settling themselves amongst the palms, Vivienne, who was not one to beat around the bush, went right to the point. "What happened in Wyoming?" Martha drew a deep breath. *Oh dear, this is what I was afraid of.* "Thomas is very curious about Whittakerville and no one will tell him anything. He is a curious young man and I feel he should be told something. This entire family is very close-lipped about that entire time in your lives."

"With very good reason, my dear." Martha was stalling, trying to pick her words very carefully. "When that dreadful man came here to kill Jeremy and the boys, I knew then that the past was going to come back to haunt us. Now Anna has run off with him to that horrible place. Oh, dear me. What can I tell you?" Vivienne saw that Martha was visibly shaken; perhaps this was not a good idea.

"I am sorry, Mother Martha but I too need to know some of what happened. I did talk to Annabelle and she said that she would appreciate your telling Thomas something about those days. Just enough to satisfy him, I am sure there will be some things he does not need to know."

"Annabelle would never do anything against Isaac's wishes. I understand why she thinks I should be the one to tell the story." Martha paused. "Vivienne, you bring Thomas here on Wednesday afternoon and I will tell both of you some of what happened. The rest, you must promise to leave alone. Do I have your word?" Vivienne assured Martha that she would accept what she was told and then leave it alone. She would make sure Thomas agreed as well. When Vivienne left, Martha went to find Jeremy. The doctor was finishing his examination.

"Your man is improving with each day, Mrs. Whittaker."

"That is wonderful news, doctor. Do you think he will be able to dance at the Summer Gala?" Jeremy smiled at his wife. Always the socialite, but what a beautiful woman she was. He wanted nothing more than to dance with her again.

"I don't see why not. I was just saying that I thought it would do him good to return to the office two days a week." Jeremy was very happy at this news; boredom was setting in. He was anxious to return to the office. He patted his newly acquired belly. All of this lying around was causing him to gain weight.

"Show Doctor Johnson to the door Martha and ask Charles to bring our lunch in the conservatory. Tell him to make mine a light lunch." Again he patted his small paunch, Martha and the doctor laughed. "I will meet you there. Good Day, doctor." Jeremy rose and walked slowly to the hall. The doctor and Martha smiled at his progress.

Jeremy waited while Martha relayed the conversation with Vivienne. "What are you going to tell her?" He knew that it would be a very difficult conversation for his wife.

"The truth, or at least some of the truth. There are certain things that shall remain buried in the churchyard with Jebediah. That young woman is very astute. The children need to know something about Wyoming, especially now that Anna is there. Everything is coming back to haunt us, Jeremy." She moved into his arms. Arms that had always made her feel safe. He held her close. *Jebediah, you bastard. Still you haunt us.* The mention of

Anna made him very sad. He missed his daughter. In spite of how much trouble she was, he loved her and wanted her home.

Wednesday afternoon, Vivienne and Thomas arrived at the mansion filled with anticipation. Vivienne was not sure which one of them wanted to hear the story more. "Are you sure Grandma is going to talk to us about Whittakerville? I thought it was a big secret." Thomas had his doubts. Vivienne nodded as Charles opened the door. Martha greeted them.

"Thomas, Vivienne, how lovely to see you both." Thomas handed a basket to Charles.

"Pa said to give you these, Mr. Charles. Fresh butter and eggs, and some apples, from the farm."

Charles bowed in thanks. "Please thank your father, Mr. Thomas." He disappeared into the kitchen.

"Please, come into the great room. Granddad has gone into the office for a few hours. There are some of your favorite cookies there on the plate, Thomas." Thomas helped himself to the cookies and then remembering his manners, put them aside and offered the plate to Vivienne and Martha. They politely refused, the three staring at each other waiting for someone to start.

"Thomas and I are looking forward to hearing about Wyoming, and we want to thank you for telling us what you can. We both understand that there might be questions you are not willing to answer." Vivienne wanted to get started.

"Well, it was a very long time ago. I was only eighteen years old. Jebediah Whittaker and I were married in England. I will tell you that I did not want to marry him. My father arranged it, and I was not happy about it. Isaac, Abraham and Ezekiel's mother had died. I was to be their stepmother. Thomas, your father, the oldest of the boys, was ten at the time, almost the age you are now. We traveled on a ship to the Americas. It was a terrible voyage.

Many people died of a mysterious illness. I was very glad to reach solid land. My joy was short lived. We traveled on a wagon train from St. Louis to Wyoming. It was worse than the sea voyage. The dust choked the life out of you, the wagons were most uncomfortable and walking was better than riding. I hated every minute of it. We arrived in Fort Laramie and then built a sod house in the place that would later become Whittakerville." Thomas asked a few questions about the sea voyage and the sod houses. Vivienne watched Martha's face as she spoke. *There is a lot more to this story, judging by the look on your face.*

"Jebediah Whittaker was the Pastor of the church. He was a kind, God-fearing man to his parishioners and they loved him. He was a monster to his family. He beat us all; he used the pioneers to his own end. He lent them money and then repossessed their farms; he was greedy, and selfish. He did not care about those people or their struggles to make ends meet. Unfortunately, he kept that information well hidden and therefore, the people of the town loved him. Jeremy and Austin traveled from England to Wyoming to find us. Jebediah had told no one where we were going, it was just by luck that they located us." She gulped air realizing that she was talking quickly. "Jebediah was killed in the church and we buried him there. The townspeople named the town after him and we left. That is about all there is to tell." Martha looked anxiously at the two mesmerized members of her family, hoping it would be enough.

"But how did he die in the church, who killed him?" Thomas was not letting this go easily.

"A robber, now that is all I have to say. Please, let this go. Your father and your uncles do not want to remember the man that beat them. I do not want to remember those horrible days in Wyoming. I have said all I care to say." Martha rose from her chair, intimating that the conversation was over. "I hope you are both satisfied now." Vivienne looked at Martha knowing there was much, much more to this story. Thomas hugged his grandmother.

"Thank you Grandma, I am glad you told me about Whittakerville. Even though Pa's father was a mean man, I am still glad they named a town after us. We are all very good people and no one has to know the rest of the story. Thank you again." Vivienne ushered Thomas to the door, she smiled at Martha but gave her a look that said, *and I will be back to hear the rest of the story.* Vivienne knew most of the story that she had just heard just from picking up bits and pieces over the previous months, but there was definitely something that was not being told. There was a big secret and it looked like the Whittakers would take it to their graves. Martha waved goodbye from the doorway, a cold shiver ran down her spine. She pushed the horror of those times to the recesses of her mind.

Riding back to the farm Thomas turned to Vivienne. He and Chestnut slowed to a walk as did Vivienne and Blackjack. "Did you think that maybe Grandma was not telling us the whole story, Aunt Viv?"

"Thomas, I think we have heard all that we are going to hear and we should leave it at that. Some terrible things must have happened in Whittakerville; things that we should not keep digging to discover. You have a good family and a good life; it appears that your Pa and his brothers were not so lucky. Now did I ever tell you the story of how my Pa and I worked on the plantation in Louisiana, picking cotton?" She told her tale to her appreciative audience for the rest of the ride home.

When she arrived home she told Abraham what Martha had said. He just nodded in silence. "Did he really die at the hands of a robber, Abe?" Abe gave her a funny look.

"If that is what Mama said, then that is what happened. Why don't you believe her?" he was irritated. She thought that strange. *What are you hiding?*

"Of course, I believe her, I just wondered if there was more to it."

"Well, leave it alone. Those days were not the childhood of dreams, more like horrible nightmares, so leave it alone. I mean it Viv, do not push this." He was getting agitated; she decided to change the subject.

"Papa Jeremy is much better, he was at the office. I am sure he is on the mend." She rose and headed for the kitchen. "What would you like for supper?" He followed her. Taking her in his arms, he apologized for snapping at her.

"I am sorry, darling. Please forgive me but my father did terrible things to Martha and us, things that do not bear repeating. I love you and I know you are just trying to understand, but some things are best left buried in the past." She kissed him and handed him the potatoes.

"You peel and I will prepare the chicken. I love you, too."

Thomas sat in the chicken coop contemplating what Martha had told them. Sissy sat next to him. "Well, are you going to tell me the story of Whittakerville?" She waited, picking at the chicken feathers on the perch. Chickens walked beneath the children's dangling feet, clucking and scratching. The two didn't seem to notice the pungent smell of chicken droppings. Thomas told her what he had been told.

"I think that old Grandfather of ours was a real bad man. Sissy, I feel sorry for Pa and Uncle Abe and Uncle Zeke. It is not nice to have a father like that. He even did mean things to Grandma, I hate him." Sissy patted him on the shoulder.

"Me too, we are never going to talk about that old meanie, ever again. Thomas, do you think Red Fox is mean like him? He didn't seem very mean when he was my friend."

"Well, he didn't seem very nice when he stabbed Granddad. I think he was just fooling us; he wasn't really our friend. The grownups don't like him much and he is their stepbrother."

"I don't understand that, how can he be their brother with a different mother?" Sissy looked confused. Thomas explained it to her.

"You know those Thompsons down by the river? Well, those boys have two different mothers but the same Pa. So they are called stepbrothers. That is what Red Fox is to Pa and our uncles."

"But the Thompson's boys Ma died and then their Pa got another wife and they had more kids. Did our old mean Grandfather get another wife and have Red Fox? Besides, Grandma isn't Pa's birth mother, the other lady in the picture in our living room is."

"I know Sissy, it is very confusing. Old meanie, as you call him was married to the lady in the picture. She was Pa, Uncle Abe and Uncle Zeke's mother. She died when they were very little. Then Old Meanie, married Grandma and she became their mother. I guess he must have married another lady after because Red Fox is his son too. Oh, I don't know the details. And from the way Grandma told the story, we never will. Let's get these eggs and get in the house before Ma comes looking for us."

"Grownups are too confusing. I think I'll just stay a kid. Come here, you little red hen." Sissy soon forgot about the conversation and went after the chickens. Thomas sighed, picked up the eggs and headed for the house.

Martha sat in her bedchamber holding the wooden box on her lap. *How long ago that was. Why must we all be reminded of those days?* She took the folded, worn letters from the box. A torn piece of silk from an old petticoat fell to the floor. Picking it up, she caressed it with her fingertips as she began to read:

My dearest Austin: My mental state could only be described as dark and depressed. All the love, laughter and joy have been replaced by endless toil, sadness and defeat. I'm mortified to say that I sometimes wish Jebediah were dead. The situation is hopeless and my life has become a nightmare. I feel my own heart filling with evil thoughts and I'm ashamed. Only the young boys keep me going. I realize that they need me for protection from their own father and I must be strong for them.

She had resolved never to destroy the letters that she had written during her time in Wyoming. The letters, never mailed, that kept her sane. Holding the worn paper in her hand, her wrist began to ache and her whole body shuddered as she remembered how it had been broken. Tenderly she replaced the torn silk and folded letters to their hiding place. That night her nightmares were filled with the face of her tormentor.

Chapter seven

The New House

As the hot sun shone on Wyoming, Anna interviewed several potential servants. Jeb had only given her one stipulation. No Indian women were hired to work in the house. She understood that his childhood has been filled with prejudice and hurt and agreed. Because of his treatment, which clearly resembled the treatment of the blacks in the south and now the Chinese in the west, the couple had no prejudice. If anything, they were both sympathetic to those treated badly by the whites. She finally decided on a Chinese couple. Anna had already hired a black woman to clean three days a week. Jeb was not keen on having live-in help, but did agree to give the Chinese couple a small cabin in the back of the property. Ling Ye was a very lovely, exotic woman with dark hair that hung down to her waist. Her husband was strong and very adept at repairing almost anything. She would cook and he would take care of the grounds and the maintenance. Chu Ying was a quiet man and although the two spoke some English, they said very little. This suited the Whittakers very well.

"Ling Ye, we are having twenty for dinner on Saturday. I will discuss the menu with you and I expect everything to be perfect. I will not tolerate insubordination or sloppy work. Do we understand each other?" Ling Ye nodded, she was just happy to finally have a job and a home of her own. Her husband had come west with the railway but soon realized his life was in great danger. The dangerous and explosive, dynamite work was done by the Chinese and their lives were of little value to the railroad men. 'Disposable', is how the railroad men referred to them. Ling Ye talked Chu Ying into leaving the railroad when the crew left Whittakerville. This job was a blessing for them both. They settled in nicely and the Whittaker house and the Whittakers were soon the talk of the town.

Anna walked proudly through her parlor. She stopped to watch the sunshine on the small garden. It made her think of St. Louis. *I hope you are well Father*. Her smiled changed to a frown. *Mother, I just wish you could see me now. You insisted I settle for Hans Kruger and his tiny house on the wrong side of the tracks, you and your rules. I will show you. I will have everything I desire. I don't need you.*

All of the furniture had been purchased from a Frenchman that was leaving Wyoming for California. She knew they had paid too much for the furnishings but she wanted them. Price was no object for Anna, as long as she got what she wanted. Jeb simply paid and let her decorate. Even he was pleased with the final result. He stood in the dining room admiring Anna's work.

French mahogany table and sideboard filled the dining room. Chairs for twenty with silk brocade upholstery lined the table. Crystal goblets glistened on the sideboard under the light of the oversized chandelier. This was the home of a fine gentleman and Jeb was enjoying every minute of it. "I must have a portrait of the two of us painted for this room Anna. I remember seeing one in your parent's mansion in St. Louis."

"Excellent idea, my love. Now are you happy with the house and the staff?"

"Whatever you want, Anna. You lead and I shall follow." She smiled. *Just the way I like it.* Jeb was proving to be the perfect mate for her, malleable, easy to lead and very generous. He took to wearing the fine clothes she bought, like a duck to water. His diction was improving, as was his writing and reading ability. Yes, Jeb was exactly the man that Anna Whittaker wanted. She walked over and placed her hand in his. He turned and smiled at her.

"Shouldn't you be getting to the railroad station? Mr. Hale will be arriving soon and we want to make sure he stays here with us. Just remember what I told you." Jeb nodded.

"Before I go, I want to give you this." Jeb took a small jewel box from his vest pocket. He handed it to Anna. She gasped as she opened it.

"Oh Jeb, it is the most beautiful diamond ring I have ever seen. Where did you get it?" He removed the large square cut diamond ring from the box and placed it on her finger above the gold band.

"Monsieur Devalle sold it to me along with the furniture. I wanted to surprise you. I know we bought the gold band in Nebraska to convince people we are married but I thought you would like to have this." She fell into his arms. Yes, Jeb Whittaker was exactly what she wanted. He held her tight. He loved her.

An hour later the train pulled into the station. Mr. William Hale, Governor of the Wyoming stepped from the train. Jeb was waiting. "Mr. Hale, your honor. May I introduce myself? I am Jeb Whittaker. My wife, Anna and I would be pleased to have you stay with us during your visit to Whittakerville. The hotel really is not suitable." Jeb picked up the man's case and pointed the way to the waiting wagon. Hale was surprised but pleased. *Well, well, a Whittaker meeting me at the train. Nice touch for a little nothing town in the middle of nowhere.* He carried his overcoat over his arm.

William Hale sat in the wagon, feeling the heat of the day. He was beginning to perspire. Jeb pointed out his many properties as they moved through town. Hale was impressed. He had to admit that he never knew there was a Whittakerville or that an actual descendent of the town's namesake existed, before this visit. But being a true politician, he acted as if the town and Jeb were the most important things in Wyoming. Jeb was surprised that William Hale was in his mid forties; he had expected a much older man. The two had a pleasant conversation. Jeb stopped in front of the hotel, just as Mr. Whitehall was leaving with several other of the town council members. The group had been discussing the Governor's visit and how it would be necessary to make sure certain facts about the accounting of the town's budget, as well as a few other indiscretions were kept secret. This was a nicely orchestrated stop by Anna Whittaker. Jeb remembered her words well, 'Just make sure your timing is perfect. Mr. Whitehall must see you with Mr. Hale. Remember we want them all to think he is my uncle.' Jeb smiled, tipped his hat at the gentlemen and moved on. The councilmen stood staring, open mouthed, as the wagon disappeared down the street. Unbeknownst to them, the messenger that they sent to the station to meet the governor, was told the train was delayed by two hours.

"Anna darling, we are here." Jeb ushered Mr. Hale into the large parlor. Anna rose from the blue velvet, high backed chair and curtsied coquettishly. Mr. Hale was enchanted with this lovely, young creature. She bowed low, letting him get just a glimpse of her low cut gown and the full breasts, it displayed. She took his outstretched hand, and smiled as he placed a kiss on her hand.

"Governor Hale, welcome to our humble abode." Her green eyes never left his. Jeb watched with interest as Anna pulled the man into her web, like a Black Widow spider, she charmed him. He was going willingly, Jeb smiled. *Men, what gullible bastards we all are. Bless you, my venomous beauty.*

Seated in the parlor, the three enjoyed tea and the conversation was lively. "I see you have Chinese servants, Mr. Whittaker. What do you think about the Chinese Exclusion Treaty, signed by President Hayes?" The question was directed at Jeb, but it was Anna that answered.

"Actually I think it is disgusting that the railroads paid the Chinese $30 per month while the white workers got $50 for the same work. I also think the government and the railway corporations were anxious to allow the Chinese into the country when they needed cheap labor, only to now limit them, because the railroad and the gold rush no longer need them." Mr. Hale was impressed, she continued. "The white man has already treated the Indians abominably. Do you not agree that this Chinese Exclusion Treaty has increased racial tensions here in the west?"

"Well, Mrs. Whittaker, I did not realize you were interested in politics. Not many women are."

"Strange thing to say when Wyoming was the first to give women the vote, Mr. Hale." Anna had strong opinions when it came to human rights including those of women. She was not one to be taken lightly.

"And in case you were wondering, our servants Ling Ye and Chu Ying have a Certificate of Residence." Jeb added, wanting to stop Anna before she lost her temper with Mr. Hale and wanting to take part in the conversation. Anna had explained the "Certificate of Residence" document, in which Chinese individuals were required to prove their residence in the United States prior to the passage of the Exclusion Act, to Jeb when she hired them.

"I didn't doubt that for a moment Mr. Whittaker and please, Mrs. Whittaker I want you to know that I was in full agreement with women having the vote. Why close to here in Laramie, women served on the jury for the first time in 1870 and I might add we had a woman, Justice of the Peace. You are in the right place if you agree with the suffrage movement." Jeb looked at Anna, her face softened. He could read her mind. *Anna Whittaker and the Suffrage movement, indeed, they haven't seen anything yet.*

Later at dinner, Anna stared at Mr. Hale several times. Finally he returned her stare, “Is something wrong, Mrs. Whittaker?”

“No, not really. You must forgive my rudeness. It is just that you look so much like my dear, departed Uncle Willy. It really is an uncanny resemblance. My apologies.” She took her lace handkerchief from between her breasts, a move he watched with much interest. Anna dabbed her eyes.

“I’m sorry to have upset you my dear, were you close to this Uncle?”

“Oh, yes, he was like a father to me. I am being silly.” Again, she dabbed her eyes. “I loved him so and I miss him. Having you here is like having Uncle Willy back.”

The three ate in comfortable silence. Ling Ye served the apple pie and tea, clearing the other dishes as she left. “We will have whiskey and cigars in the gentlemen’s room, Ling Ye.” Jeb nodded to Anna.

“Yes gentlemen, if you will excuse me, I must freshen up. Enjoy your brandy, Uncle Willy.” She feigned embarrassment. “Oh dear, please forgive me. How silly of me. Of course, I mean Governor Hale. Oh dear, how embarrassing.” The governor patted her hand.

“Don’t be silly my dear, I find it charming. Please don’t fret.” He laughed. Jeb joined him. After winking at Jeb, Anna flitted from the room. “What a charming creature, you are very lucky, Mr. Whittaker.”

“Jeb, please call me Jeb. Yes, Anna is definitely a charming woman. She does miss her uncle very much. I apologize for what just happened.”

“No, no Jeb, my good man. No apologies necessary. I found it rather flattering. Now shall we go and have those cigars and whiskey, and please call me William?”

Jeb moved them toward the back of the house and the room that was now the gentleman’s room. A large billiard table graced the center of the room. Dartboards were mounted on the west wall and a large, well-stocked bar took its position on the opposite side of the room. A huge fireplace, with logs perfected staked, greeted them. Large windows and ceiling fans, gave the necessary ventilation. Mr. Hale took in the room appreciatively. "I have some questions about Whittakerville that perhaps you can answer. I do have a meeting in the morning with the town council. Will you be there?"

"Me? No, I am not on the council."

"Well, why not, man? You are a Whittaker and this is your town. Politics don't interest you?"

"Actually we've only been here a few months and have just gotten settled. But you know, I might be interested in a position in the politics of this town." Hale nodded in agreement while selecting a fine cigar from the wooden cigar box. " I don't mind telling you that the Indian and the Chinese situation disturb me very much. I abhor any race related violence." This was a new thought to Jeb. *Mayor Whittaker, I can just see it now*. He smiled at the thought.

"It's settled then Jeb, you will accompany me tomorrow." The two men lit their large cigars. They picked the whiskey from the tray and let the warm liquid slide down their throats, warming them on this starry Wyoming night.

The following morning, Anna, Jeb and Mr. Hale had breakfast in the hotel. The men were to meet the town councilmen at 10. Once the other gentlemen had gathered, the three entered the meeting room. Anna, making sure she was in earshot of Mr. Whitehall, kissed Jeb and then turned to Mr. Hale saying loudly, "See you later, Jeb, Uncle Willy." She held her hand to her lips to appear embarrassed and whispered. "Oh dear, I have done it again." Mr. Hale laughed and waved as she left the room. The other men in the room did not miss the reference. Anna had achieved the desired effect. Jeb was proud of her. The others looked at him with confusion as she left the hotel, why was he still here?

"Gentlemen, I have asked Jeb Whittaker to join us. I believe you will find him taking a bigger role in the politics of Whittakerville in future. I am sure you all agree with me that he would make a fine candidate for mayor." The men stared back in shock but no one showed their disapproval. Hiding their surprise, swallowing this new development nearly choked them. Hale looked from one to the other. They all nodded in agreement, giving each other sideways looks of shock and reluctance. "Now, let's get down to business."

Governor William Hale happily boarded the train the next morning and never returned to Whittakerville. Anna Whittaker waved goodbye from the windy platform with a very content look on her lovely face. Jeb held her hand proudly. They would now begin to plan Jeb's political career, but there was no denying which one of them would be running the town.

The town councilmen were in an uproar. "First they hire Chinese, when we are trying to rid the town of the yellow scourge and now, he is going to run for Mayor. This is an outrage." Mr. Whitehall, thinking he would be the only candidate for Mayor, was furious.

"Well, you heard the Governor, he wants Jeb Whittaker as Mayor. I for one am not about to argue with her "Uncle Willy." Several others nodded. "We will just have to think of some way to make sure he doesn't win the election." Some of the men in the back of the room laughed out loud.

"That won't be hard, since it will be us counting the votes." The others joined in.

"As far as the yellow scourge goes, we can scare them out of town. It worked with the last bunch that set up here. I agree with the Workingman's Party of California, they just come here and steal jobs from decent white folks. Who wants to take on the yellowbellies?"

"I'll gladly drive them out of town. Leave that job to me." Joe Baker smiled through broken front teeth. The others toasted him with their ale.

"Now about Whittaker." The meeting went on long into the night before a solution was agreed upon.

Several days later, Ling Ye arrived home with her clothes filthy and in tatters. "What happened to you?" Anna took the basket of food from her shaking hand. "I asked you what happened?"

"Nothing, Ling Ye fall down. No problem Missy. No problem." Ling Ye moved toward the kitchen but Anna was persistent.

"You did not fall down. Now, I demand an answer." Finally after much persuasion, Ling Ye told Anna that a man attacked her as she left the general store. He dragged her into the alley and hit her several times. The man told her to take her husband and leave town, before they were both killed.

"Who was this man, give me his name." Anna was furious. Ling Ye did not know who the man was. A large blue bruise began to form on the woman's cheek; her lip was cut and bleeding. Anna sent Ying Le to her own cabin to clean up and change. She went to find Jeb.

"I'm telling you Jeb, it is those bastards in the town council. They are as crooked as they come. I want you to do something about this now. I will not have them drive my servants out of town and I will not allow them to intimidate us." Jeb was growing agitated. Memories of many beatings he had as a young child came flooding back. The white man had not been kind to Red Fox, the half- breed. The more Anna ranted, the more agitated he became. He picked up his coat and went to the study for his knife.

"I'll be back shortly." He slammed the door as he left. Anna stared after him. *You won't drive us away you bastards. You don't know whom you are dealing with.* She went to find Ling Ye, not out of concern but to make sure dinner was being prepared.

John Little was the town snitch. John was slow mentally and everyone teased and taunted him. He hid in corners and saw things. If you wanted to know anything, just give John Little some candy or a beer and he would spill the beans. He didn't miss much. Jeb found John outside of Smithers' blacksmith shop. "I want to know who hurt Ling Ye, my woman servant. Tell me now, John." Smithers stood leaning his large frame against the doorway listening. Jeb nodded to him.

"It was the one with the broken teeth that did it." John snatched at the bag of candy, Jeb looked over to Smithers.

"Thanks John, you can go now." Jeb and Smithers walked into the blacksmith shop. "The one with the broken teeth?"

"That will be Joe Baker, he is a bad bastard. One mean son of gun." Smithers told Jeb how the town had been slowly taken over by the town council and how the townspeople were not happy about it. There had been several unexplained lynchings over the past few months. "You be careful Jeb. You don't want to make enemies of those men."

"No one hurts my staff and gets away with it Smithers, I appreciate your help. Now forget this conversation ever happened." Jeb went to the local saloon to look for Joe Baker. He found him coming out of the saloon. Jeb followed him to the alley, on feet as silent as the night. Moments later in the alley between the saloon and the general store, Joe Baker lay with his throat slit. Jeb walked calmly into the saloon, sat down and ordered a beer. No one saw a thing.

When he returned home, Anna asked him what he had done. "Did you find out who did this?" Jeb nodded and poured himself a whiskey. “I think you have had enough already, now tell me what happened.”

“It is taken care of, that is all you have to know. Now call Ling Ye and Chu Ying in here. I have something to say.” He gulped his drink and took a seat by the fireplace. Anna soon returned with the two frightened servants.

“The Whittakers do not tolerate bad treatment of our servants. I want you both to know you will be safe working here. If anyone threatens you again, please come and tell me right away. Do I make myself clear?” Jeb paused and looked at them. They stood with their heads down, eyes on the floor. “The man that hurt Ling Ye is not going to hurt anyone else, ever again.” At that, Chu Ying looked into Jeb’s eyes, he said little but an understanding passed between them. He made a short bow.

“Thank you, Bossman.” He turned and taking Ling Ye’s arm escorted her from the room. Anna watched as Jeb poured another whiskey.

“Do you want to tell me what happened?”

“Nothing for you to concern yourself with. It is done. Just know that I have taken care of it.” Anna put her arms around him and squelched her desire to know more. She trusted him. She would not ask.

Chapter Eight

Mothers and Daughters

Martha stared out the window as the sun peaked from behind a cloud. The entire garden was illuminated with a lovely glow. She was remembering how happy Jeremy was the day she told him she was pregnant with Anna. *Anna my daughter, did I fail you? Is it my fault that you have turned into this selfish, self-absorbed woman? Or are you just evil like your uncle, Jebediah Whittaker? Oh dear God, what were you thinking? Running off with a total stranger, a man that tried to kill your own father.* What was Martha feeling, was it guilt or love, hate or remorse? Her feelings toward Anna were not clear. Martha shuddered as a chill ran down her spine.

"Thinking of your lovely summer roses, my Dearest?" Jeremy walked over and rested his arm on her shoulders. She turned toward him, kissing his cheek.

"No, just thinking. How are you feeling today?" She moved toward the breakfast table and poured Jeremy's tea. The scent of lemons rose towards her nostrils reminding her of another time long ago. She had been eighteen and her father had just told her that she was to marry Jebediah Whittaker. Again she shuddered.

"What is it? Are you ill?" Jeremy took the cup from her hand. "Martha?"

"Oh, no I just remembered something I have to do at the shop. Do you mind if I don't sit down to breakfast with you? I will just take a muffin with me." She kissed the top of his head and rushed from the room. He watched her go, wondering what could be so important. He sipped his tea, thinking of his day ahead.

Martha arrived at the Haute Couture after Loretta. She removed her cape and hat as she entered the office. Hans was busy with the ledgers. "Good morning Hans, where is Loretta?" Martha went to look for her in the sewing room.

The two checked the latest shipment of silks and taffeta and then moved to the showroom. Racks of gowns hung along one side, a burgundy settee sat in the middle of the room. A table held the catalog of the latest designs and two dainty chairs completed the lounge area. The two women sat on the settee. "I don't know what to think about Anna." Martha looked at her friend for advice.

"You know she is not my favorite person, Martha. What are you feeling?"

"That's just it, I don't know. Guilt, love, hate, confusion? I just do not know what I feel when I think about Anna. She is so stubborn and headstrong. I know Jeremy is very concerned about her."

"Martha, the letter you got said she was fine and knowing Anna, I am sure she is."

"That letter was received months ago. I wish, for Jeremy's peace of mind, she would write again. I don't feel that she is in any danger; I just don't know what to think or what to feel. I'm her mother, for heaven's sake, I should be upset, missing her, something!" Martha put her head in her hands; the strain was beginning to show. Loretta hugged her friend but offered no comment. Loretta knew exactly how she felt about Anna and that was angry. Angry at the girl for putting Martha and Jeremy through this torture, angry at Anna for sending David away, angry because Anna was nothing but a selfish, self centered little brat. *Thank you, God for my Abby.*

"Why, even Christmas went more smoothly because Anna was not here. She always caused trouble over one thing or another, honestly Loretta. I feel terrible, but to be honest it was nice to have a day without the drama and the problems." Loretta had to agree, even Abby had commented months earlier, how pleasant the day was without Anna.

"Martha, you must let this go. Don't feel guilty about Anna; you did your best. We have no control over how our children turn out. All we can do is guide them and pray for the best."

"Oh God, Loretta, I keep remembering the night Anna miscarried. She was fifteen, for God's sake. She lied about having sex; she looked me right in the eye and said she was never with a man. How could she have expected me to believe her? She never would take responsibility for anything." Martha wiped a tear away. "You know Loretta, I was so angry that I couldn't even comfort her knowing the pain she was in. I am afraid guilty is exactly how I feel."

"Well, talking David into lying for her and claiming he was the father didn't endear her to me Martha. I think Anna should take all of the responsibility for that situation."

"You are so lucky to have a wonderful daughter like Abby, Loretta."

Almost on cue, the doorbell tinkled and Abby Wells walked into the shop. A hot blast of air followed her. "Mother, Aunt Martha, are you here?" Hans hearing her voice appeared at the office door.

"Good morning, Abby, you look lovely today. Is it still hot outside?"

"Yes, it is very humid, Hans. How are you? I am looking for my mother."

"The two of them went out back to supervise a shipment. You will find them there, or you can wait here with me if you like." Hans was hoping she would stay.

"Thank you, Hans, I will go and find her." Abby liked Hans but she knew that he wanted more from her. She was in love with Ezekiel and that was that. *If you don't marry me Ezekiel, I will be an old maid for the rest of my life.* Abby disappeared behind the door and Hans reluctantly returned to his work.

Abby found Loretta and Martha still seated on the settee in the showroom. "Mother, would you like to go shopping this afternoon?" Loretta smiled at her daughter. Martha looked at the two of them with envy. *Why can't I have that relationship with my daughter?* Loretta finished her work and she and Abby set of to shop. Martha helped Hans with the books until closing time.

Abby wanted to ask her mother about her situation with Ezekiel. Loretta tried to help her but it really was up to him. He would have to make the next move. Just as they arrived home, Ezekiel walked up to the gate. "Good evening, Ladies, may I help you with your parcels?" Elegantly he scooped the bags from their hands and ushered them to the front door. "May I speak with you in private, Abby?"

Abby and Ezekiel went into the living room while Loretta took the parcels upstairs. Quietly, she returned to the top step where she could eavesdrop without being seen.

"I have to return to England. I was supposed to leave at the end of next week. I have done a lot of thinking Abby." Abby held her breath. She prayed that he would ask her to go with him.

"Yes, Ezekiel, what have you decided." Under the cloth of her flowing skirt her fingers were crossed. At the top of the stairs, Loretta too held her fingers crossed and prayed.

"It was necessary for me to make a change in my travel plans. It appears I can not travel with the new ticket next week, but will have to wait until the end of the month."

"Change your ticket? I don't understand." Abby was becoming more confused by the minute.

"The new ticket is for two, Abby. Will you marry me?"

Suddenly, Ezekiel dropped on one knee. He produced a beautiful diamond ring; a single diamond surrounded by green emeralds.

Abby stared at him. “Yes, yes. Oh my darling, Yes.” She almost knocked him over as she leapt into his arms. He carefully placed the ring on her finger, before picking her up and twirling her around the room.

“I know I put you through it, Abby but I had to be sure. I am a bachelor at heart and I would never want you to be hurt. I love you with my very soul.” He kissed her. “You will have to come to England with me, that means leaving your family. You understand we will have to marry in the next week, so it will be a very small affair.”

“Of course, Ezekiel, anything you say. Oh, I love you too.” Loretta was elated but heartsick. *Next week, you must leave me, my dearest Abby. Dear God how will I stand losing both of my children?* Slowly she walked down the stairs, holding her head high. *I must not let you know my heart is broken.* Abby ran to her mother, hugging her tightly.

“Oh Mother, I am so happy. I know you wanted a big wedding but Ezekiel has just asked me to marry him and go to England at the end of the month. My dream has come true. Please be happy for me, Mother.” Tears of joy ran down Abby’s face, Ezekiel watched as Loretta forced a smile. He knew that Abby’s leaving would be a difficult time for the Wells family. He would come back and speak to Austin later.

“My Darling, I will go and start planning our wedding. I shall return after dinner and we can discuss it with your parents. I must tell Mama and Papa. Remember, I love you.” He pecked Abby’s cheek, placing his hand supportively on Loretta’s shoulder; he left the house. *Why did one person’s happiness have to make another so miserable?*

The next few days were a whirlwind of activity at St. Louis Haute Couture. The seamstresses worked overtime. "She will have the most beautiful wedding gown Martha. Although we have little time, we must make this special." Loretta chose the finest lace for the neck of the gown. "Martha, are you sure we should use this lace, it is most expensive. Austin and I appreciate your gesture of giving Abby this dress, but we really do not want to take advantage."

"Loretta, you are the best friend any woman could have. I love Abby as if she were my own daughter." A sad expression crossed Martha's face. "I probably will never be able to do this for Anna, this is my pleasure."

Abby's school friend, Stephanie McEachern stood admiring the gown that she would wear. "Abby you are so lucky to have your gowns made here. This shop is the envy of everyone at school. I love this design for your gown, with the removable panel."

"The removable panel will be taken off after the ceremony. I like the idea of the chaste and pure bride with the high neckline, later revealing the true woman beneath." The two young women giggled like schoolgirls. Martha and Loretta smiled.

"Oh, Abby, it is too bad you will miss my wedding next spring. England is so far away." Stephanie looked forlornly at her friend.

"Yes, it is far away." Loretta added sadly.

"Mother, please we have talked about this." Abby went to her mother and hugged her. "I know you will miss me, and I, you, but this is my life now." Loretta looked over Abby's shoulder at Martha, who understood only too well what losing your daughter felt like.

Vivienne was fitted for a Matron of Honor's dress. Stephanie was bridesmaid. Even little Sissy was included, wearing her flower girl dress from Abraham's wedding.

"Sissy, Grandma will make you a new dress for this wedding, if you like."

"No Grandma, I really only need one dress, I don't really like wearing dresses. But, thank you anyway." Annabelle shook her head.

"What will I do with you, Sissy?"

"Just love her and enjoy ever minute that you have her with you. One day she will grow up and leave." Annabelle knew that Martha was thinking of Anna. She hugged Sissy close. "We will alter the dress to fit our new bigger, Sissy." Everyone laughed.

Isaac and Abraham, as best man and usher, completed the wedding party. They helped console the nervous bridegroom. "Are you sure you are making the right decision, Zeke?" Abraham wanted to be sure Zeke was ready to settle down. "There will be a lot of unhappy young ladies in this town."

"Oh, I am very sure this time Abe, I love Abby and I want her for my wife."

The day of the wedding, Jeremy was thrilled but could not help remember the last wedding. He sat in the church with Martha; a cold chill ran down his spine. *I might have died here.* Martha knew what he was thinking and squeezed his hand. The music began to play. Vivienne walked down the aisle with Sissy, both dressed in pale purple gowns. Stephanie followed in the palest of green, which set off her chestnut hair beautifully. Abraham, Isaac and Ezekiel stood proudly at the altar. Ezekiel wore the most up to date shorter style coat, with narrow lapels closing higher at the throat, almost covering the tie.

Loretta turned with tears in her eyes as Austin walked Abby down the aisle. Ezekiel gasped at the sight of her. Her gown was white silk, a simple, straight empire waist gown. A lace gusset rose high on her neck, sparkling jewels on the lace reflected the light. Long tight lace sleeves hugged her arms. Lace gloves appeared as if they were one with the sleeves. The left glove had a split seam on the ring finger for ease of placing the wedding band without removing the glove. The lace veil was feminine, held in place with a diamond tiara. Her hair was pulled back and high on her head. Small blonde tendrils fell from the fringe over her lovely, beaming face. She was the most beautiful bride in the world in his eyes.

I wish David could have been here, Loretta could not help but think of her son so far away in the Navy. Grandma Minnie smiled as the young couple said their vows. She had waited years for this day. Thomas sat in pew beside Minnie with his baby sister, Amy. Agatha Carruthers, now in a wheel chair sat holding Amy's hand. Agatha was as close to a mother as Martha could have and she was thrilled to see these two families coming together. Agatha loved Ezekiel as if he were her own grandson. Agatha looked over at Martha. Martha glanced over and smiled but Agatha could see the sadness in her eyes. *You are thinking of your own daughter aren't you Martha?*

The couple was married without incident and a small reception at the Whittaker mansion followed.

"Anna has missed her brother's wedding." Martha stated. Annabelle and Vivienne looked at each other. "I am sure this will only be the first of many events that Anna misses in this family. She no longer cares about any of us."

"Mother Martha, I am sure Anna cares very much for all of you. She is just far away, that's all. Don't distress yourself." Vivienne was trying to appease Martha but she had to agree with what Martha said. Anna didn't seem the least bit interested in writing to let them know what was happening with her or in finding out how any of them were. In an effort to change the subject, Annabelle suggested they go and see the blushing bride and the three made their way across the room.

"A married man, Zeke. I never thought we would see the day." Isaac patted his brother on the shoulder. "You are a lucky man."

"Abby is too good for you, my brother," Abraham added. Abby smiled at the brotherly jousting going on. She loved this family. Austin came to dance with his daughter, pride shone in his eyes. Ezekiel took Loretta's hand and led her to the dance floor.

"Aunt Loretta, I know you are heart broken. I am so sorry to have to take Abby away to England, but I must return to work. The school has been very understanding but their patience has run out." She smiled at him.

"I know Ezekiel, I know. It is just hard to let her go. She has loved you since she was a child and now you are her knight in shining armor. Take care of my girl." Tears ran down her face. Ezekiel reached into his pocket and handed her his handkerchief. He was close to tears himself.

"I almost lost her Aunt Loretta. I am sorry it took me so long to come to my senses. I will take very good care of her and you and Uncle Austin can come and visit anytime you like." Loretta told him she considered him family, although they are not related. The families grew up together. She trusted him and she knew her daughter would be safe.

The families enjoyed the festivities. Jeremy and Martha watched their sons; now all married, with pride. "You did a wonderful job with the boys Martha, I am very proud of you. You were saddled with three stepsons, at the young age of eighteen and now look at them. Happy, successful and strong, all thanks to you." He kissed her and she put her arms around him. *If only I had done as well with our child, Jeremy. Our daughter, whose wedding we will never have the pleasure of attending.*

"I will miss Ezekiel when he returns to England. It has been nice having all of them together again, but he has been away from the school for too long." Martha would miss her son a great deal but she knew he had to go. At least Abraham and Vivienne had decided to settle in St. Louis instead of returning to Louisiana. Thomas arrived to ask Martha to dance; she curtsied and let him lead her onto the floor. Isaac and Abraham soon joined Jeremy.

Sissy arrived moments later. “Dance with me, Granddad.” Jeremy picked her up and danced away. The rest of the family watched and smiled. Austin stood with his arm around Loretta’s shoulder; they would miss their lovely daughter very much.

At the end of the month, after a tearful goodbye, Ezekiel and Abby took the train to Boston. From there they would board a ship to England. Loretta cried for days.

Chapter Nine

Mayor of Whittakerville

"Anna, you have to realize how the whites feel about half breeds. If anyone ever found out that I was Red Fox, half-breed son of Jeb Whittaker and a Cheyenne squaw, they would probably lynch me. We have to be very careful."

"Jeb, you look very different than you used to. You can do this, Jeb. Sign your name and you will become a candidate in the election. We will do our best to get everyone in town to vote for you." She brushed a speck of dust from his jacket. "In the meantime, I will dig up as much dirt on Whitehall as I can."

"I don't know Anna. I don't think you understand what prejudice and hate can do." Jeb paced nervously. Too many memories haunted him. The attack on Ling Ye brought it all back to him in vivid detail.

"My brother Abraham went to Mississippi and Louisiana to be a doctor to the blacks after the war. I have heard many stories of the cruelty of the whites. We always treated our black servants with respect and they were paid, never slaves. My family is very empathetic to all races." She watched him pace. *You don't look like a half-breed; you look white. I must convince you.* "Our servants have good accommodations and good pay, you defended Ling Ye when some lunatic attacked her. Although that is something else no one should know about. You were careful?"

"Of course, I was careful. No one saw me, you can be sure of that. Oh all right, give me the damn paper and I will sign it. I hope you know what you're doing, Anna."

Meantime down at the hotel, Whitehall and several of the other town council members were having a meeting. "I'm telling you, his wife picked up the application this morning. Whittaker intends to run against you Whitehall. I for one am not happy about it." Several of the others nodded in agreement.

"Then, we will have to make sure he meets with a terrible accident." Mr. Whitehall was sweating profusely, he was nervous. "One of you will have to make the arrangements, I have to keep my hands clean until after the election." He was remembering the look in Jeb's eyes the day he came for his fortune. *That man is a very dangerous madman. Yes, we have to eliminate him.*

Jeb delivered the documents and went to the saloon to announce his candidacy. He was met with cheers and claps on the back. It seemed the townsfolk had been praying for someone to run against Whitehall and his hoodlums that called themselves the town council. Several men offered to buy Jeb a drink, or help in anyway with the campaign. Jeb was feeling better, for the first time in his life he felt like he was accepted, like he belonged.

Later, after too many drinks, Jeb left the saloon. He walked toward his home at the far end of town. He was not drunk but his head was fuzzy. Little did he know he was being followed. Surprised from behind, someone hit him on the back of the head. His vision went blurry and then he blacked out. He was dragged behind the sawmill. A large wooden door slid open. The smell of rough- cut lumber filled the air. Two men bound his arms. A gag was tied around his mouth. Jeb slowly began to gain consciousness. His head throbbed. His vision was blurred. Realizing that he could not move his arms, terror began to settle in. One man left the scene leaving the other alone with a very frightened Jeb. "Goodbye Whittaker, nice knowin' ya." The man laughed a cruel and heartless laugh. The second man, the much larger of the two grabbed Jeb roughly. He tried to clear his muddled mind, staring at the multitude of wide round blades, covered in sharp teeth hanging on the wall. Shelves filled with oilcans, rags, and hand tools slowly came into focus. Piles of sawdust loomed on the floorboards like tiny mountains in a desert of dust. He shook his head but his vision would not clear. He was being jostled like a rag doll, by this huge man. Suddenly, Jeb found himself standing on a crate, a rope tight around his neck. He squinted his eyes tight, trying to focus. Strange thoughts filled his head. *Where is everyone? Why is the sawmill empty in the middle of the day?* Jeb tried to fight but his arms were tied tightly behind his back. Terror filled his every pore, sweat dripped from his face. "Why are you doing this to me?"

"Ready to meet your maker, Whittaker?" The man spat on the dusty floor. He kicked the crate from under Jeb's feet. The rope tightened, he felt his breath leave his lungs, as his weight pulled downward. His airway was being choked off; he was dying.

Just before blacking out, he felt someone grab his legs, lifting him in the air. The rope slackened quickly as if cut from his neck. Jeb gasped for air, he choked. Cough after cough as he pulled air into his lungs. He was placed gently on a bale of straw. Recovering, he turned to see his assailant lying on the ground. Over him stood, Chu Ying with a very large blade, dripping with blood. Jeb was never so happy to see anyone in his life. Chu Ying released Jeb's arms and removed the gag. He simply smiled, nodded his head and waited for Jeb to lead the way home.

"Chu, I am forever in your debt. Thank you, my man, how did you know where I was?" Jeb wiped his sweating brow with his handkerchief and brushed the dust from his clothing. He gulped several large breaths of air trying to calm himself.

"Chu Ying follow Bossman, you okay now, Bossman?" Jeb nodded and extended his hand. Chu Ying hesitated but then he reached out and shook Jeb's extended hand. Jeb looked up to see the rope swinging from the rafters, the noose was still around his neck. Slowly he lifted it over his head, dropping it on the body of his assailant.

"This man is on the town council, and so is Mr. Dillon, the owner of this sawmill. It is funny but I wondered where everyone was. Strange things go through your mind when you are being murdered." Chu Ying nodded. They dragged the man's body behind a large pile of logs and left it there. "Someone else can finish this job. I am sure there are enough men that knew about what was happening here today." They walked home silently; a new bond was formed. Jeb knew that Chu Ying would watch his back and it seemed that his timing was perfect.

"Oh my God, Jeb, they tried to kill you. This is terrible. These men are very dangerous, first they threaten Ling Ye and now this." Anna was beside herself. "Thank God for Chu Ying, I didn't even know he was gone." Jeb explained what happened and then told Anna that he was more determined than ever to become the mayor of Whittakerville. She saw a new determination shining in his eyes. She was very pleased. Twenty-year-old Jeb Whittaker was becoming his own man.

Anna knew that she must not do anything to make him feel he was making a mistake, she needed him proud and determined. "Darling, we will show those horrible men. They will learn that Jeb Whittaker is not a man to trifle with." She kissed him but her thoughts were not of him. *By this time next year, I will control this town. You my dear Jeb will be the mayor but I will pull the strings. So stay determined. Little do they know, the more they attack you, the more determined you will be. Together we will make this town ours. I will work on the women.* An evil smile crossed her lips. She hugged Jeb tightly. He felt safe in her arms.

Anna invited twenty of the most influential women of Whittakerville to tea. She fussed over the room and the food. This was very important to her plan. Anna screeched when Ling Ye knocked the vase of flowers over. Ling Ye bowed her head, becoming accustomed to the tirades of her mistress. Slowly, she bent and retrieved the vase. Anna shook her head in disgust, left Ling Ye and went to get dressed. An hour later she heard voices and decided to make her entrance. She had dressed very carefully in her new gown. Slowly she ascended the staircase, ready to meet the women that would ensure her future. As she reached the parlor, only two women were seated there. She looked anxiously around the room. The older of the two rose to greet her. "Mrs. Whittaker, how nice of you to invite us." Anna recognized her as the old woman from the cemetery. *Great, one old bat and the town spinster, where is everyone else?*

"Mrs. Mueller, how lovely of you to come. And Miss Parker, nice to see you." Elegantly, Anna extended her hand to the two women intimating that they sit down. "Are the others coming?" She maintained her poise beautifully.

"Actually, we are the only two. I am afraid the other's husbands forbade them to come. You will soon learn that there is a certain group of men that control this town, my dear." Anna was fuming but the smile never left her face.

"Miss Parker, I understand you would like to be our new school teacher." Miss Parker fidgeted nervously. Her handkerchief twisted in her long thin fingers.

"I am afraid, Mr. Whitehall has decided to send for someone else, Mrs. Whittaker. I am working in the general store right now." Alice Parker's eyes never left her hands.

"That is preposterous, I know that you were chosen from a very extensive list of applicants. Why on earth would Mr. Whitehall want someone else?"

"Very simple, He is hiring his cousin from back east. Easier to manipulate, although what kind of threat this poor creature poses is beyond me." Olga Mueller spoke directly to Anna, and then looked at Alice with sympathetic eyes. She reached over and patted her hand.

The ladies were served tea and cakes and treated like aristocracy. Anna soon realized that Olga Mueller was a great source of information and not one to be pushed around. She decided to make her an ally. Where Miss Parker would fit in was still a mystery, but since they were the only two in attendance, Anna was sure to make very fast friends with them both. Anna asked Alice more details as to why she did not get the job of schoolmarm. Anna knew that the town had hired her. Alice had traveled a long way. Something didn't make sense and Anna wanted to know the details. Alice was hesitant but after a few minutes of prodding and some motherly reassurance from Olga, Alice told her story.

"I arrived in Whittakerville filled with anticipation of a long awaited school of my own. I studied very hard and obtained excellent grades. I did teach for two years back east before I applied for this job. Mr. Whitehall met me at the train and escorted me to the hotel. The next day he appeared at my door and although I did not invite him in, he entered the room nonetheless." She paused to catch her breath. Her handkerchief twisted violently in her hands. Anna waited while the nervous young woman sipped her tea.

"He tried to kiss me. I pushed him away but he wanted more. He ripped my blouse and I ran from the room and hid in the broom closet." The young woman trembled.

"What a pig, the devil himself that man." Anna was shocked. She patted the other woman's hand. Alice was only a few years older than Anna but appeared very innocent. It was obvious that Anna was the more mature of the two. ”Please go on, my dear.” *So Mr. Whitehall, you do have secrets.*

“There really is not much more to tell. The next morning one of the town councilmen arrived and told me that the job was being given to someone else.” Alice wiped her eyes. “I spent my savings to travel to Wyoming. I didn’t have any money to get back east. Olga was nice enough to offer me a job.” Olga looked from one young woman to the other. She could see that Anna was not about to let this injustice continue. A sense of respect was beginning to grow for this young impetuous woman. Olga knew just how ambitious Jeb and Anna were but perhaps they would get Whittakerville back to the lovely town it had once been.

Later that evening, Anna paced her room like a wet hen. Jeb returned home to find her there. “What has you all upset?”

“Upset, I am not upset. I am furious. I invited twenty women for tea today, twenty! Do you know how many showed up? Two.” She paced faster, her face set in a stubborn frown. “Our illustrious town council forbade their wives from coming. Forbade them!” Her voice rose, “Do you hear that? Unbelievable!” She was angry and Jeb knew better than to remind her that he told her she was expecting too much. He sat on the chair by the dressing table and watched her. Jeb was growing used to seeing Anna in an agitated state one-minute and sweet as pie the next. She was a paradox. “Our memorable Mr. Whitehall tried to obtain sexual favors from poor Alice Parker before he would give her the teaching job. That man is a pig. We have to do something.” After several minutes she informed him that they were going to church in the morning.

“Church? I don’t think so Anna. I am not going into that white man’s church. Do you know what those missionaries did to my mother’s people?” He was certainly not going to church, no matter what her reasons.

"You listen to me. Do you want to be the mayor of Whittakerville or not?" She glared at him. "We are going, you don't have to listen to the sermon, just smile at the ladies and tip your hat. Religion is the least of my concerns but we want to appear pious. Religion worked for your father, it will work for us." He winced at the mention of Pastor Jebediah Whittaker. "We are going." With that she marched from the room leaving him shaking his head in frustration. He didn't like the reference to his father. *Anna you are beginning to scare me*. Sometimes she was so exasperating.

The next day was a bright, sunny, Sunday. Typical for this time of year and everyone's mood was light. Anna, dressed in her finest, smiled and greeted everyone with a smile. Jeb tipped his hat and smiled right along with her. She purposely seated herself next to Mrs. Smithers, the blacksmith's wife. A tall willowy woman with graying hair, Mrs. Smithers was not included in the earlier luncheon invitation as she had been out of town. Further down the pew, sat Mrs. Bolton, the wife of one of the town councilors. After introductions were made, Anna invited the two women for lunch. Mrs. Bolton was about to decline when Anna mentioned how preposterous it was that 'some of the town's women were being controlled by their husbands'. Anna added that such intelligent women should take pride in having their own opinions, after all Wyoming did give women the right to vote and hold very prestigious positions. Mrs. Bolton thought for a moment and then with a most determined expression, accepted the luncheon invitation.

"Tell me Mrs. Whittaker, what are your thoughts on temperance?" Anna smiled, gathered her thoughts carefully before she replied. Realizing she was in the church and most of these women probably were in favor of temperance, Anna knew to measure her reply carefully.

"Why as you know Susan B. Anthony was first and foremost one of the pioneers of the Temperance movement. She is truly the woman that I most respect and try to emulate. Of course, Frances Willard the leader of the National Woman's Christian Temperance Union is another of my heroines." Mrs. Bolton, surprised at the apparent knowledge of this young woman, was most impressed with the mention of the Woman's Christian Temperance Union. Anna had a new friend.

Mrs. Smithers smiled over to her husband. This was a very wise young woman. She also accepted. He had discussed the Whittakers with her earlier, making note that if anyone could make changes in this town, it was Mr. Jeb Whittaker. She had agreed to get to know the intriguing Mrs. Whittaker better.

After church, Mrs. Bolton was seen arguing with Mr. Bolton outside the church. Anna smiled, *One down, seventeen to go.* Taking Jeb's arm, she whispered, "All this talk of temperance, I could use a good stiff whiskey." He laughed out loud as they walked down the street.

Anna visited the school on Monday as the children were dismissed. "Do you have children, Mrs. Whittaker?" one of the mothers inquired.

"Why no, but Jeb and I plan to have a family one day. I just love children." Anna smiled. She was becoming a very convincing liar. She chatted with the mothers, planting the idea that Miss Alice Parker was a well-qualified teacher and should start immediately. The schoolmaster was leaving in two days. "The education of our young people is paramount in this town. I think we should all have a meeting this evening and tell the mayor we demand that Miss Parker be hired. You ladies are aware of Susan B. Anthony and the National Woman Suffrage Association. I am arranging for Mrs. Esther Hobart Morris, Wyoming's first woman Justice of the Peace and a member of the National Woman Suffrage Association to visit this town. I would be thrilled to have all of you hear her speak." After her carefully spoken, most inspiring tirade, she had the women riled up. For someone with no children she knew exactly what to say to make these women feel that their children were being denied a good education. The women all agreed to meet that night at the school.

Two days later, Alice Parker rang the school bell. Anna Whittaker walked her to the schoolhouse personally and smiled as the children greeted their new schoolmarm. Alice fussed and fidgeted, thanking Anna profusely. Naturally, she thought Anna did it for a sense of justice and fair play. Anna, who had her own motives, was very satisfied with the outcome. A small boy bumped into her, she shrieked. Recovering quickly, she feigned surprise, smiled, patted his head and sent him on his way. *Little brat, watch where you are going.* Alice watched Anna with interest, but said nothing.

After that Anna concentrated on the Quilting Society, the Book Club, the Church Ladies Auxiliary and every other group of women that she could infiltrate. Susan B. Anthony and the National Woman Suffrage Association, and the Temperance Union, became prevalent in her talks. The more she spoke of women's rights, the more entrenched she herself became. Anna became a magnet for information in the news, in books and any other source she could find. Having learned that the esteemed ex-Justice and women's rights activist would be in Fort Laramie, Anna sent a telegram to Esther Hobart Morris inviting her to Whittakerville. Reading that Mrs. Morris was once a dress designer, Anna mentioned that her husband was related to the famous owner of the St. Louis Haute Couture. She also mentioned being enthralled with the women's right movement and that she felt the women of Whittakerville needed to hear more.

Olga Mueller sung Anna's praises to everyone that came into the General Store. She was pleased with the outcome at the school. Olga also thought that Anna Whittaker was a very determined young woman who believed in equality. She wondered how Jeb Whittaker was related to Martha. Olga had known Martha many, many years before when she lived in Whittakerville. One day she would ask him. The years were creeping up on Olga and her memory was fuzzy at times, but she was sure there were only three sons when Martha left Wyoming.

Three weeks after the first invitation to tea, Anna Whittaker entertained thirty women in her parlor. At the end of the long dining table sat Esther Hobart Morris, retired Justice of the Peace. Before the ladies arrived, Anna discussed the St. Louis Haute Couture, gushing proudly over the fact that Mrs. Morris knew of Martha Whittaker. Naturally, Anna did not tell her that Martha was her mother or that she and Jeb were cousins and not a married couple. *You do have your uses, Mother. If name- dropping works, I will use everything I have to, to get what I want.* Anna smiled at Mrs. Morris. The older woman was very impressed with Anna Whittaker and her husband.

Jeb, on Anna's instruction removed all of the alcohol from the house. She reassured him that it would be brought back as soon as the ladies left. Jeb didn't really understand Anna's reasoning, but he cooperated fully. She never let him down. He was suave and sophisticated as he greeted the ladies; they were charmed. He could not believe the way Anna could produce well-known politicians at the drop of a hat. She amazed him.

Anna introduced Mrs. Morris, telling the ladies that Mrs. Morris held tea parties much like this one years before, in order to convince the legislature to give women the vote. The afternoon went very well, the women were impressed. Anna was happy that her plan was coming together.

In the hotel, another meeting was taking place. The men were not so impressed. "I am getting pressured at home, to vote for Whittaker,"

"Who wears the pants in your family, Frank? Whittaker is not going to be mayor. We will make sure of that." Mr. Whitehall had noticed the change in the attitude of the townspeople toward him. He too was getting nervous. The town had been his for three years and he liked the power. Not to mention the money that he and the councilmen siphoned from the town's budget. No, he was not about to give this up without a fight.

"Well, you had better think of something soon, Whitehall, because I might wear the pants but I won't be getting any sex if my wife is not happy." A few of the others nodded in agreement.

"Oh, for God's sake man, get one of the saloon girls to take care of it. Now what are we going to do about Whittaker?"

That night the cabin that Ling Ye and Chu Ying lived in, was set on fire. Fortunately, Smithers, Jeb and Chu Ying put the fire out before it spread to the big house. The volunteer fire department did not come, although the bell sounded loud and clear.

Ling Ye and Chu Ying moved into the Whittaker's house. Anna referred to it as "the devil's work" when she told the women at the Ladies Auxiliary the next day. "Something has to be done about this town before all of us are killed in our beds. We need a mayor that will take back control." The ladies agreed but many were frightened. Anna played on their fear.

Anna visited the grave of Jebediah Whittaker. *Tell me your secrets. You didn't amass such a fortune without being very clever. You were right about using religion to manipulate the masses.* She stood staring blankly at the head stone, a cold, icy wind blew across the churchyard. The wind blowing through the trees made a sound like someone laughing, she looked around curiously. Anna laughed. She visited often, the grave became an obsession with her.

Jeb and Smithers talked with some of the men and many agreed that something had to be done about the town council. Although they could not come up with a plan, one of the men filled with a false bravado, publicly challenged Mr. Whitehall. That night the poor man was found hung from a large tree just outside of town. Everyone knew who was responsible but the sheriff was on the council. He would not listen to the protests. The townspeople grew silent. The fear was palpable.

The election was three weeks away. Jeb and Anna plotted. In the end, Olga Mueller provided them with some very valuable information. Apparently John Little, the town snitch had found some papers that Mr. Whitehall had left burning behind his office. John had put the fire out and brought the charred remains to Olga. Olga realized the value of the unburned evidence. She traded John some chocolate for them and called Anna right away. Anna visited the lawyer's office, where a letter addressed to Gov. William Hale, along with the unburned papers, was shown to Mr. Whitehall. Anna informed him that 'Uncle Willy' had been telegraphed and was on his way to Whittakerville. She also informed him that the ex-Justice of the Peace and her very good friend, Esther Hobart Morris would be returning as well. Anna mentioned that Mrs. Morris would be very interested in talking with Alice Parker. The lawyer turned pale. With sweat pouring down his face, he agreed to resign. After the visit by Anna, Whitehall miraculously withdrew from the mayoral race and left town.

Several of the other town councilmen decided to travel to Utah or California on unexpected business. Some packed up their families and fled, others simply left their unsuspecting wives in Whittakerville. Even the sheriff resigned. The following week, the election was held.

"What happened Whittaker?" Mr. Smithers congratulated Jeb, who was declared Mayor of Whittakerville. "Why did Whitehall leave town in such a hurry?"

"Let's just say, some evidence came to light that he didn't want the people to know about. Now let's have that beer. And someone buy one for John Little." Jeb was proud of himself; he could hardly believe all that had happened to him since he came to this town. He remembered how his entire childhood had been spent filled with hatred. Never did he dream he would come this far. He was filled with a new sense of confidence. He knew he owed it all to Anna. "Smithers, I want you to serve on the town council along with me. We also need a new sheriff." The party was a huge success.

The ladies of the Temperance Union stood to the side discussing Jeb's drinking. Anna assured them that it was just to celebrate his victory. Three women whose husbands had abandoned them after the town council scandal approached Anna. "We want to thank you for introducing us to Mrs. Morris. She has made all of the arrangements necessary for us to claim all of our husband's property here in Whittakerville, as our own. We owe you a debt of thanks, Mrs. Whittaker." Anna blushed graciously, hugging the women. She thought about her own conversation with Mrs. Morris. Anna had inquired as to her position in the town council if something happened to Jeb. Would she be able to step in as acting mayor, if anything terrible happened to him? Mrs. Morris assured her that a number of widows had stepped into their husband's political roles in the past few years. Anna also had her draw up and witness Jeb's will, convincing Jeb to sign it. *Just a little assurance, my love.* The people of Whittakerville celebrated Jeb's victory. John Little, town hero, wiped his filthy face and slurped his beer. Anna smiled at Jeb, the new mayor of Whittakerville, Wyoming.

Chapter Ten

The News

"Abe, I have to tell you that I am very upset that Vivienne went to Mama about Wyoming. That part of our lives has been dead and buried for years and I for one, want it to stay that way." Abraham could see the tension in his brother's face. He too was upset with Vivienne, but he understood that she was trying to placate Thomas. Martha seemed willing to tell them both some of the story, which made Abraham feel better about the whole situation.

"Honestly, Isaac, Mama said she told them enough to satisfy them. She didn't seem upset." Abraham placed his patient files in the drawer and took his seat behind the large desk. His brother paced the small office. "Besides, with our dear sister, Anna in Wyoming, this may not stay buried for long. Talk about a strange twist of fate." Isaac turned and stared at Abe.

"Fate? More like the devil's doing. Just finding out that our father had another son was shocking enough, without Anna running off with that lunatic. I tell you Abe, I could strangle him with my own hands for what he put this family through." Isaac's face was crimson, he was very angry. Abraham tried to calm him down.

"Listen, we don't know if we will ever see either of them again. If that fortune was as large as Jeb Jr. said, then the two of them are probably heading for the Gold coast by now. Anna always was trouble, now she has someone just as evil as she is, to share her life."

"That's a little harsh, Abe. I wouldn't call Anna evil." Isaac was distracted from his initial anger. "She was troublesome, but she is also at that age. I remember all of us giving Mama a hard time when we were teenagers."

" That sounded more like Annabelle than you. We were just happy to have a great life in St. Louis and be away from Wyoming and our father. I don't think we were troublesome at all. Speaking of trouble, have you had a letter from Zeke yet?"

"No, but I think he and Abby will be very happy together. She worships the ground he walks on." Almost as an afterthought, Isaac added, "I believe he has settled down."

"I hope so, I wouldn't like to think that poor Abby's heart would be broken because Zeke could not be faithful. Not like us, eh brother?"

"One man, one woman suits me just fine. Now, how about that coffee you were promising me for fixing that broken door?" The brothers left the medical office and headed for the kitchen.

Back in St. Louis, Martha sat in the parlor holding a newspaper. Arthur Langley sat opposite holding a china teacup in his weathered hand. "I hope I did the right thing in bringing that newspaper to you, Martha. You and I have known each other since Wyoming. I thought long and hard before I knocked on the door." Martha had met Arthur on the wagon train to Wyoming more than twenty years ago, not only was he a friend, he was Loretta Well's father. Now in his late sixties, Arthur had retired from the wagon trains but still bought and sold horses. Most of the wagons were used for freight now that the railroad reached the west coast. He still had many connections in the business.

"How did you get this, Arthur?" She could hardly believe what she had just read. Jeremy arrived home before Arthur could answer.

"Martha, where are you?" Jeremy hung his coat in the hall and proceeded to the parlor. "Arthur, how nice to see you." He walked over and shook Arthur's outstretched hand. "What a nice surprise. Oh, a hot cup of tea is exactly what I need after the cold wind out there, fall seems to be in the air already." Jeremy picked up the teapot and poured himself a steamy cup of tea. Martha looked troubled. "Arthur, is something wrong?"

Martha answered before Arthur. "Darling, Arthur has brought us a newspaper from Wyoming. Although it is a month old, it contains some very interesting news. I think you should read it for yourself." She handed the neatly folded paper to her husband. He took his spectacles from his pocket. He began to read.

Moments later, he looked at the pair in shock. "Is this true, Arthur?"

"I am afraid so Jeremy, Jeb Whittaker Jr. is now the mayor of Whittakerville and Anna is apparently, his wife. I'm sorry if this upsets you but I thought you should know."

"Thank you, yes, any news is good to have Arthur. You have a daughter, I am sure you understand how I feel." Martha looked up at Jeremy. She had not missed the 'I' rather than 'we' in Jeremy's statement. Jeremy avoided her gaze. Arthur stood, thanked Martha for the tea and left the house.

"So it appears my newly acquired nephew is now my son-in-law, and the mayor of Whittakerville. Well, well, well, this is an interesting twist of fate. I think I need a brandy." Martha didn't say a word; she simply walked to the cabinet and poured a large brandy for Jeremy and a sherry, for herself. *So you do know how I feel about our daughter, Jeremy. Oh my dear, I wish I could feel some sadness but I don't. I don't miss her at all.* Martha's hand was shaking as she set the tray on the small table.

"I think we need to gather the family together, please call Charles." Jeremy swallowed the brandy in one large gulp. *Married, and I didn't even get to walk you down the aisle, my darling daughter. I hope this man is not like his father. I pray he is not.*

Isaac and Annabelle arrived first with the children. Abe and Vivienne were close behind. Charles showed them into the dining room, where the huge table was set for dinner. The children climbed into the large oak chairs anxiously awaiting the abundance of food they have grown to expect. Jeremy and Martha walked down the stairs and greeted their family. Both had a very serious look on their face. Isaac and Abe exchanged a glance. Jeremy seated Martha, took up his place at the head of the table and signaled for the rest of them to take their seats. Something was not right, the tension was apparent.

"We have called all of you here to give you some news about Anna. Apparently, she has married Jeb Jr." Several gasps could be heard. "That is not all, we have learned that they have taken up residence in Whittakerville and Jeb. Jr. is now the mayor." The name evoked dread on the faces of Isaac and Abe. Thomas grew excited. Vivienne, who was seated next to him, grasped his hand to keep him from blurting out. But it was Sissy that spoke first.

"So Auntie Anna married Red Fox, the Indian?" Annabelle shushed her. Jeremy looked around the table at the people he loved.

"Yes Sissy, but he is not Red Fox the Indian, anymore. He is Jeb Whittaker, the mayor of Whittakerville." Everyone stared at him in shocked silence. The food grew cold.

"Fate brings many strange things into our lives, history often repeats itself. We just pray that Anna will not have to suffer as all of you did. Anna stated in her letter that Jeb. Jr. was not a monster and that stabbing me was an accident." Martha rose from her chair and stood behind Jeremy, giving the impression of a united front. "Perhaps Jeb. Jr. is not whom we think, but a good man. We can only pray that he treats her well." Jeremy looked at his family. Isaac looked away. They all nodded in agreement, all except Martha. She was lost in her own thoughts. *Jeb might not be a monster but I am not so sure about Anna, my love. Time will tell.*

The following week, Vivienne was working on Isaac's farm. She wiped the dirt from her face, dusted off her work clothes and headed for the house.

"Hi Annabelle, mind if the hired help has a cup of coffee?"

"Viv, come in. You know I can never get used to you wearing pants. I know they are practical but working at St. Louis Haute Couture since I was ten, I still think ladies should wear dresses." Vivienne just laughed and left her dirty boots at the door.

Vivienne sat in the kitchen of the warm, cozy farmhouse. "That was quite a shock learning that Anna is married to Jeb.Jr." Vivienne picked up her cup and stared blankly over the rim. Several loaves of freshly baked bread cooled on the counter, making the kitchen smell inviting.

Annabelle pushed stray red hairs back in place as she checked the oven. "I don't know what to think." She placed the warm cookies on the table. "Careful, they are hot."

"Smells delicious. What do you think about Anna?" Vivienne picked at one of the cookies with her fork. It crumbled. "Oops, too hot."

"I can still see Martha's face when she handed me that letter. There was one word that was blatantly missing, the word 'love'. Anna didn't sign it 'love Anna.' No mention of loving Jeremy and she never said she 'loved' that Indian." Annabelle went over to check on the sleeping Amy. "Sorry, I mean Jeb. Jr. Isaac always calls him that 'crazy Indian' and I am afraid that is how I think of him."

"I think of him as the bastard that almost dragged you into the woods, to do heaven knows what. Days later, he grabbed me and then beat me senseless, out on the road. If Isaac hadn't come along, he probably would have killed me. I still think Jeb. Jr. or that 'crazy Indian' is a madman and Anna better watch out." She ate her cookie. Crumbs fell on her trousers; she brushed them onto the floor.

"Viv, the children. You really must watch your language." Annabelle loved Vivienne but sometimes the young woman was very coarse and uncouth.

"Sorry, you and Mother Martha will make a lady out of me yet." Viv laughed.

"I am actually surprised that someone didn't suggest going after her. I know Jeremy is beside himself; he really misses her. Isaac and Zeke offered when she first left town, but no one has mentioned it again." Annabelle took the chair opposite Vivienne.

"Martha doesn't seem very upset about her leaving. Forgive me for saying so but I almost get the impression that Martha is happy she is gone. I never really got to know Anna before our wedding. Just a few snippy comments from her now and then; I can't say as I liked her much." Vivienne reached for another cookie, offering the plate to Annabelle.

"Anna has always been a handful but mothers and daughters sometimes have rocky relationships. I am not sure how Martha feels, as a matter of fact, I don't think she knows how she feels."

"My mother died when I was young but if I ever have a daughter, I will love her to pieces, especially if she is like Sissy."

"Something you are trying to tell me?" Annabelle raised her eyebrows.

"No, not yet. But hopefully I will be pregnant soon. I would love a houseful of kids." The two wiled away the afternoon discussing the family and their futures.

Thousand of miles away in England, Austin and Loretta visited their daughter and Ezekiel. "How wonderful to have you here with me, Mother. I have missed you so." Abby was thrilled. She showed Loretta the parlor, decorated in moss green, gold, rust and earthy tones. The furniture was large and stately. Loretta commented on Austin's study. "It is so like him. I can just picture him sitting here amongst his books. You are very lucky to have such an elegant home, Abby. It thrills me to see you both so happy."

Austin and Ezekiel toured the grounds and Austin was most impressed. "Years ago, Martha and I played in that meadow as children; too many years ago to remember. It has been years since I was back in England. This is a lovely stately home you have Ezekiel, and Abby seems perfectly at home here."

"Yes, she is the perfect English wife. Everyone loves her. She is tutoring some of the boys at my school. Did she tell you?" Ezekiel showed Austin the large formal gardens. The hedges were trimmed, some in the shape of birds or animals.

"That is wonderful news. Abby was a brilliant student; I want her to use what she learned. It was wonderful of Jeremy to give Loretta and I this opportunity to come to England. He didn't want to leave St. Louis, in case there was word of Anna."

"Still no word, bloody hell? What is wrong with that girl?" Ezekiel seldom cussed but he was angry with Anna. "Excuse me, Austin. She makes me so angry."

"I am afraid I have to agree with you, Zeke."

"Hopefully she will write to him again soon. Unfortunately Anna always was a self- centered girl. I am sure both Mama and Papa are frantic with worry." Arriving at a large cluster of buildings, Austin pointed to the left. "The stables are this way." Saddled horses awaited them. The men took a ride out into the grounds.

Abby and Loretta toured the house and Loretta could see how happy her daughter was. It made her feel better.

"We must go into town and I will show you the lovely English tearoom there, Mother." The two women spent days together enjoying each other's company and making the most of their time together.

"I have a letter from David. He is doing very well in the navy. I wish he could have been at my wedding. Has there been any word of Anna?"

"Not a word, Martha and Jeremy are beside themselves. Daddy brought them a newspaper saying that Jeb. Jr. was now the mayor of Whittakerville and he and Anna were married. That girl is too much. Let's talk of better subjects shall we. Any pitter patter of tiny feet in the near future?" Loretta looked at her daughter, Abby laughed.

"No, Mother but you will be the third one to know." Loretta and Austin were content and happy to see their daughter blissfully settled.

After a blissful two weeks, they traveled by ship, back to America, feeling better about their daughter and son-in-law's future. They would still miss her, but it was time to let her go.

Chapter Eleven

Illness Strikes

"Missy, come quick. Bossman fall down." Ling Ye was frantic. Anna rushed into the dining room where Jeb was sprawled out on the floor.

"Jeb, are you alright? Jeb." Anna shook Jeb but got no response. "Go for the doctor, hurry up." Ling Ye stood frozen to the floor. "I said, 'Go you stupid woman."

Ling Ye ran from the room. As soon as the door closed, Anna walked calmly away from Jeb and looked out the window. Autumn was arriving with a flourish. The grass was turning yellow and the leaves were blowing on the trees. Several leaves drifted to the ground. She stood there until she heard the door and then quickly moved back to Jeb.

"What seems to be the problem?" The doctor quickly checked Jeb. Anna stood by, looking frantic. Ling Ye watched her suspiciously.

"Let's get him up to the bedroom. Where is your man servant?" Without being told, Ling Ye went to find Chu Ying. Jeb was placed in bed as Anna questioned the doctor nonstop.

"I am not sure, Mrs. Whittaker, we will have to wait until he comes to. Perhaps he can answer a few questions in the morning. His breathing seems to be regular. Just stay with him through the night and I will come back in the morning." Anna showed the doctor to the door. She walked calmly to the kitchen.

"I will have my supper now." Ling Ye gave her a strange look, and went to fetch the meal for her mistress. Later she took Chu Ying outside for a private conversation. Anna watched them from the window. *Just what are you talking about. It looks very serious. Perhaps it is time to terminate this employment agreement.*

The next day the doctor concluded that Jeb had severe stomach pains. All he could say was that Jeb must have contracted food poisoning. Jeb was conscious but very ill. He vomited most of the day. Ling Ye continually provided a clean pail and several cool drinks. She wiped his fevered brow, fretting over him. Anna went shopping with Alice Parker. Although she found the plain, mousy young woman dull, Alice made Anna feel superior. Whenever they were together, gentlemen always paid a great deal of attention to Anna, ignoring poor Alice completely. This suited Anna very well. The ladies of the town also seemed impressed that Anna and Alice were friends, and Anna was going to do whatever she had to do to achieve her elevated status in Whittakerville.

"How is your husband today? Does the doctor have any idea what is wrong with him?" Alice fidgeted in her seat. Anna looked around the hotel to see who was there.

"What?" She was not paying the least attention to Alice.

"I asked you how your husband was feeling today." Alice was used to being ignored. All of her life she was the A student, the girl that the boys avoided. Her parents treated her more like a servant than their daughter and fawned over her sister, who everyone said was beautiful. The harder Alice tried to get good marks and be the perfect child, the more everyone adored her sister.

"Oh, he just has an upset stomach. I'm sure he will be up and about in no time. That reminds me, I must stop by Jeb's office and finish up some paperwork. Come on, let's go." Alice found Anna's lack of concern rather unnerving but she remained silent.

Ling Ye looked pale when Anna returned. "What's the matter with you? Are you getting sick now?" Ling Ye shook her head.

"Ling Ye with child, Missy. No problem."

"No problem! The last thing I want is some screaming brat running around this house. Go to Fort Laramie and get rid of it or I will get rid of you." Ling Ye stared at her in shock. "You heard me, I will take you there myself. There will be no children in this house."

Ling Ye ran frantically from the room, Anna watched her go, shrugged, and picked up her paperwork. As far as she was concerned, the matter was settled.

For more than a week, Jeb lay in his bed. Anna sat with him for a few minutes each morning and then using the excuse that there was pressing mayoral business to take care of, she left. He was happy that she was making sure his duties were taken care of in his absence. Chu Ying visited his room often; he and Ling Ye would stare knowingly at each other. Jeb wondered what was going on. Ling Ye avoided Anna as much as possible; she was frightened that Anna would take her to Fort Laramie or fire them.

Two weeks later, Jeb was back in his office. He sat discussing his health with Bill Smithers and Donald Martin, the new town sheriff. "What do you think it is?"

"I am not sure, Doc thinks it's food poisoning." Jeb shuffled some papers on his desk. It appeared that Anna had taken care of business very well in his absence.

"Food poisoning? Do you think it is something that your dad blamed servant made? Shoot man, you had better be careful the servants aren't trying to kill you." Donald laughed, the other two appreciated that he had a suspicious nature. He was a big man, moving his tall frame often trying to get comfortable. Smithers liked these two young men; he knew they could be great friends. Although he was old enough to be their father, the three always found a common topic of conversation.

"Chu Ying and Ling Ye are like family, they would never do anything to harm us. No, I think I just got some bad meat. I will be fine." The other two men looked first at Jeb and then at each other. They were not convinced. Suddenly, Jeb doubled over; severe stomach pains overtook him. Bill and Donald rushed to his side. His assistant ran to fetch the doctor immediately. Donald and Bill took Jeb home.

"I don't understand it, perhaps there is something wrong with your drinking water. Do your wife or your servants show any signs of distress?" Jeb shook his head. The doctor was puzzled. He ordered Jeb to bed. For days he suffered clammy sweats, severe diarrhea and vomiting. Several nights, he was delirious with fever. Ling Ye stayed by his side. This time it took longer for him to recover; thankfully Anna took care of all of the town business in his absence.

"Darling, I am so pleased that you step right in like you do. You are an angel. Soon people will start thinking you are the mayor." Jeb chuckled, smiling at Anna. She reached over and pushed a stray lock of hair out of his face. He was very pale.

"Jeb, dearest. You know you will be back in the office soon, I am just helping out. You are the real mayor of Whittakerville." She fixed his blankets, kissed his cheek and then excused herself. As she approached the kitchen she heard raised voices.

"I told you it was her. I saw what she did. You have to do something before Bossman is dead." *My, isn't this interesting. So you think you know something do you, Ling Ye? I think you and I will take a little trip before the week is out*. Noisily she approached the kitchen.

"Mr. Whittaker will have his lunch now, Ling Ye. Chu Ying don't you have work to do? I will be at the office." With that, she marched from the kitchen leaving the two servants staring after her. Her total lack of concern was evident. Ling Ye turned to Chu Ying, her expression told him they could not wait.

Anna closed a deal with the railroad to reroute the train line so a storage yard could be built in the town. It would mean a great deal of money for Whittakerville and a nice bonus for Jeb, in the way of a land sale. She, of course, did not refuse the beautiful diamond brooch that the railroad executive gave her. He was determined to close the deal before Jeb came back, knowing that Jeb was against it. Jeb owned several small cottages at that end of town. The rail line would have to go through the poorer section of town, demolishing these cottages. This meant that several families would be left homeless. Anna did not care about that. She held the brooch up to the sunlight admiring its' sparkle. The railroad brought much prosperity to the towns along the track. Anna could imagine Whittakerville growing over the next few years. The final papers were signed and delivered to the waiting railroad executive that afternoon. She rushed off to a meeting with the new Whittakerville branch of the National Women's Suffrage Association.

Chu Ying rung his hat in his hands, nervously waiting in the Sheriff's office. Finally, Donald Martin arrived. "What can I do for you? Your Whittaker's man, aren't you?" Chu Ying nodded. He was hesitant to speak. Bill Smithers arrived, rushing into the room as if he were expected.

"Sorry I'm late, well what do you think, Donald?" Donald gave him a perplexed look. Chu Ying looked up and shook his head. "Tell him for heaven's sake man, tell the sheriff what you told me. Come on, don't be frightened." Bill went over to stand beside Chu Ying.

"What the hell is going on?" the sheriff was getting anxious.

"Missy poison Bossman." Chu Ying was a man of few words. The sheriff looked at Smithers wondering if he understood what the man was trying to tell him.

"Missy? You mean Mrs. Whittaker? She poisoned Mr. Whittaker? You had better have proof because the Whittakers are powerful people in this town." Smithers signaled for him to let the Chinese man finish. Martin, who had great respect for the older Smithers, walked over and took a seat.

"Ling Ye saw her put something in his soup. Later she did it again, only this time in gravy. She no eat gravy." The sheriff pondered this information for a few minutes.

"What did she put in his food? Maybe it was just salt." Chu Ying reached into his pocket and produced a bottle.

"Arsenic! Doggone it man, this will kill poor Whittaker. Are you absolutely positive?" He began pacing the small sheriff's office. "How do I handle this one?"

Both Donald and Bill Smithers knew that Anna Whittaker was well respected and becoming a powerful force in the town. It could mean his job if he was wrong. Could he take the word of a servant? "Shoot, let me think about this. Don't say one word to anyone. Do you think Mrs. Whittaker knows that Ling Ye saw her? If so, your wife could be in danger."

"We'll come back tomorrow, Donald. I understand your problem. Whatever you decide, I'll back you up." Smithers ushered Chu Ying from the room. The young sheriff put his head in his hands. Jeb Whittaker hired him; he owed the man. Not only that, he liked him. What was he to do; he couldn't let Jeb Whittaker be poisoned. He was hired to uphold the law.

Chu Ying returned to the house to find Ling Ye in tears. Anna had ranted and raved about the meal and then fired her. Ling Ye told him Anna threw the entire contents of the soup pot across the room like a madwoman. He took his wife to their tiny room and started to pack the few belongings that they had. Silently, they left the Whittaker house and went to Bill Smithers blacksmith shop. He gave them the little back room and told them to stay out of sight. Smither was worried for their safety. Bill's wife told him that Anna was becoming very demanding with the women, almost totalitarian. Several of the ladies had left the Suffrage group because of her. There had been other instances at the dress shop in town that were most disturbing as well. After she related several odd occurrences over the past weeks, Bill knew he had to tell her. He hesitated telling her about the poisoning but in the end, he did tell her, swearing her to secrecy.

"You must get Mr. Whittaker out of that house right away. She is trying to kill the poor man. Oh dear, dear, dear. That woman is insane." Mrs. Smithers was beside herself. Her husband convinced her to wait until the next day. He too wondered if it would be too late.

Jeb felt much better this morning. The sun was shining brightly. It was starting out to be a fine day. The night before Anna had been very amorous with him and he felt wonderful. He found his way to the kitchen. "Ling Ye, I would love bacon and eggs this morning." He stopped dead at the sight of a complete stranger in his kitchen. "Who are you? Where is Ling Ye?"

"I'm Clara, your wife hired me yesterday. Apparently the yellowbellies ran away with the silverware." Her rotund body shook when she laughed.

"First of all, if you are going to continue working here, we do not use terms like 'yellowbellies' and Ling Ye and Chu Ying would not steal anything. Where is my wife?" Jeb was furious. He didn't like Clara and he wanted some answers. He turned on his heel and left the kitchen. "Anna, Anna."

"Stop shouting like a commoner. I'm right here." Anna was putting on her coat.

"Who is that woman?"

"That woman is our new cook. Now calm yourself or you'll get sick again."

"I demand to know what you have done. Where is Chu Ying?" He was very angry. His whole body shook.

"Your dear friend, Chu Ying took off with our silver candlesticks, my best silver brush and mirror and some money. They were nothing but thieves, so good riddance. Now I have work to do, are you coming?" She dismissed him as if he was a child and he didn't like it. He grabbed her arm.

"Let go of me this instant." Anna's face grew stern and angry. She tried to pull her arm away but he held fast. "Let me go, you stubborn ass."

"Not until you give me some answers." Suddenly there was a loud knocking on the front door. The distraction was all Anna needed to free herself. She rushed to the door, finding Alice Parker standing there.

"Anna, I must speak to you about these changes you want in the school curriculum. I really don't think we should be teaching this to the students. They should make up their own minds about things like this." Anna grabbed the poor woman's arm and moved her down the steps.

"We can discuss this at the school. Do not forget who is responsible for you having this job, Miss." She turned and gave Jeb a very angry look, before proceeding down the street. He was fuming. Donald Martin rode up to the front door on his stallion, as Jeb watched Anna walk away.

"Whittaker, we need to have a chat." Martin dismounted and following Jeb's angry stare, saw Alice and Anna walking away. "Problem?"

"No, just a household spat, come on in Donald." Jeb ushered Donald into the parlor. "What can I do for you? Would you like a cup of coffee?"

"How long is your wife going to be? This is a very confidential conversation." Jeb looked at the sheriff strangely. He pointed to his study and the sheriff followed him.

"Now exactly what is this about?" Jeb was very curious and still angry from his run in. The sheriff dropped a large pillowcase on the floor. It clanked when it landed. Jeb stared at it curiously. "What on earth, is this about?"

"John Little found this in your trash. He took it to Olga, because last night he saw the young Chinese couple in the street, carrying all of their belongings. John thought they might have dropped this, so he picked it up but he couldn't find them. He knew Olga would give him chocolate for something this valuable, so he took it to her. Olga called me." Donald emptied the contents on the floor. One silver mirror and hairbrush, two silver candlesticks and several spoons clattered together in a heap. Jeb just stared.

"Little found this in our trash, you say?"

"Yep, no doubt about it. Somebody threw it out last night and I know where Chu Ying and Ling Ye are if you think it was them. Your wife fired them." Jeb's head jerked up.

"Fired them! She said they ran off with the silver. Wait until I get my hands on her. Chu Ying saved my life. The man is my friend." He stood up; his whole body was shaking. Over the past month he had lost a great deal of weight, his strength was waning. He grabbed the back of the chair. Donald wished he didn't have to tell him anymore. He could see that the man was already suffering.

"You better sit down, there is more. Crap man, this is hard for me to tell you." Donald finally found the words and told Jeb about Chu Ying's accusation. Jeb refused to believe it. Donald assured him it was true.

"I checked with the doctor and he said your symptoms all definitely point to arsenic poisoning. He gave me a written statement. I don't want to accuse your wife, Whittaker but the facts are all pointing in that direction." Donald reminded him of the way Anna had taken over the mayoral duties in the past few weeks. He also told Jeb what Mrs. Smithers had said about some of the women quitting the association. "She is spending a lot of time in the church cemetery. Olga thought that was strange." The pieces started to fall together. Jeb sat with his head in his hands.

"I need to talk with Chu Ying and Ling Ye, where can I find them?" He looked up at Donald, who felt terrible delivering such news to a friend. Donald tilted his head in the direction of the door. Jeb stood, still not wanting to believe his friend.

Donald, put on his hat and headed for the door, with Jeb close behind. Together the sheriff and Jeb rode to the blacksmith shop. The two young Chinese stood with their heads down when they saw Jeb. He approached them slowly.

"I have come to apologize for my wife's actions. Please tell me what you told the sheriff. Chu Ying, you saved my life once, I trust you explicitly. Please, tell me what you know." All three sat on wooden chairs facing each other. Chu Ying was hesitant, but told Jeb about the arsenic, about Anna throwing the soup pot and how she fired them.

"Just want be sure you okay, Bossman." Jeb didn't want to believe it, but he knew in his heart, it was true. He had trusted her explicitly and she had betrayed him. Jeb extended an outstretched hand and Chu Ying shook it. The two stared into each other's eyes for several seconds.

"Looks like you have saved my life once more. You will have your jobs back shortly; please stay here where you are safe. Donald will deal with Anna." Jeb turned to Donald who stood listening to the exchange. Jeb ran his hand through his hair hesitating.

"Sheriff, do your duty. I believe Anna Whittaker tried to kill me and by the way, she is not legally my wife." Donald nodded and left the blacksmith shop. He knew how hard this must be for Jeb. Bill Smithers, who was in the next room, jerked his head around in surprise at Jeb's last statement. Jeb stayed staring at the floor in utter disbelief. *I actually loved you Anna, I loved you.*

Anna Whittaker shrieked at the top of her voice. She tore the bed sheets to ribbons. She threw the metal dishes at the bars that held her. But no one paid attention to her. Life outside her jail cell continued.

Jeb Whittaker sat in his office. The past week had been very difficult for him but the town stood behind him. He had many friends here. At long last, he had the respect he desired, but at what cost? The one and only person he had loved and trusted had betrayed him. Not only had she lied to him, but tried to kill him. He could not understand it.

Picking up a piece of official Whittakerville stationary, he wrote a letter to Martha and Jeremy:

Dear Mr. And Mrs. Whittaker

This letter is to inform you that Anna; your daughter has been arrested for attempted murder. If you want to come to Wyoming to see her before her trial at month end, you must hurry. She will be sentenced to death by hanging if found guilty. I know that you do not feel kindly towards me, however I treated your daughter with the utmost respect and even love. She returned this by trying to poison me. I am sorry to give you such news.

Yours truly,
Jeb Whittaker
Mayor of Whittakerville, Wyoming.

P. S. Mr. Whittaker, I must apologize for hurting you, I was a very angry young man and am a much different person now. Surprisingly I owe it all to Anna.

Chapter Twelve

The Truth

The letter arrived in St. Louis on a bright sunny autumn morning. Charles delivered it with the other mail to Jeremy's study. After breakfast, Jeremy sat at his desk scanning the mail. He picked up the letter noting the return address, Jeb Whittaker, Mayor, Whittakerville, Wyoming. Curious and hoping it was a letter from Anna at long last; he sliced the envelope with the silver letter opener.

Jeremy stared at the paper before crumbling it into a ball and throwing it against the wall. He put his head in his hands and began to weep. Martha found him like that a few minutes later. She rushed to his side. "Jeremy what is it? What has happened?" He pointed to the crumbled ball. Slowly Martha walked over and picked it up, dreading what she would find. She straightened the paper and read Jeb's words. All of the color drained from her face. She stood frozen in place. *Dear God in heaven, this can't be true. Anna, in prison, about to be hanged. Oh Dear God.* Her knees began to buckle, she grabbed the back of the chair for support.

Jeremy regained his composure. "Charles, Charles." He called the butler instructing him to send a message to Abraham and Isaac immediately. He also requested that the Wells family be called. Martha tried to console him but he told her to leave. "Let me be. I need to be alone." Heartsick, Martha walked up the stairs to her room.

Martha cried, cursed Anna, cried some more and then tried to compose herself for the dreaded evening that was about to unfold. Jeremy had informed her that the truth about Whittakerville would be told. No excuse, no more secrets. It was time to tell the family the whole truth. She knew better than to argue with him, but she did not want to experience all of the pain over again. She did not want Isaac and Abraham to go through that horror again. She lay alone on her bed, sobbing.

It was not long before the entire Whittaker family and Austin and Loretta were seated in the dining room of the Whittaker mansion. Everyone looked confused and very concerned. Martha and Jeremy entered the room together.

“I am sorry to have to call all of you here, but we have some very bad news.” Martha looked over her family, tears formed in her eyes. Jeremy took control.

“I want everyone to eat their supper and then we will go into the parlor where you will hear all of the details. Thomas, you are going to hear all about Whittakerville. I know you have been anxious to hear for a long time but we had our reasons for not talking about those days. Unfortunately, now the truth must be told.” He looked from Isaac, to Abraham and Martha. She stared at him with tear filled eyes. "The entire truth." Austin and Loretta exchanged a concerned look.

Annabelle reached for Isaac’s hand, Vivienne turned toward her husband. Both men were solemn. The family ate in silence. Sissy could not keep quiet any longer. “Is this going to be like one of Aunt Viv’s stories, Granddad?” Jeremy shook his head and continued to eat, seated at the head of the table. Martha was nervous, picking at her food. Everyone ate in silence.

An hour later, the family was seated in a circle around Jeremy and Martha. The maid took baby Amy up to the nursery. The children sat on the floor restlessly awaiting the family history. Jeremy turned to Martha and signaled her to begin. Loretta and Austin sat to Jeremy and Martha’s right.

“A very long time ago, I was an eighteen year old girl. I lived in England with my father. One day he told me that I was to be married to a man, ten years older than me with three sons." She paused and looked from Isaac to Abraham. "I did not want to marry him and I did not want to be a mother." Tears filled her eyes; she patted them with her handkerchief.

"After the wedding, Jebediah Whittaker, his boys, Isaac, Abraham and Ezekiel and I traveled on a ship to America. There was a terrible disease on the ship and many people died. I wanted off that ship. I tried to escape but Jebediah found out and he stopped me." Isaac and Abraham looked at each other. They had not known this.

"Is that why he beat you, Mama?" Abraham reached out and held Martha's hand. "We didn't know." She nodded.

"Yes, he found out and he beat me very badly. The boys were told to wait in the corridor outside the cabin." Jeremy reached his arm around her shoulders for support.

"What a big meanie, someone should have thrown him overboard!" Sissy shouted. Annabelle calmed her and motioned for her to be quiet. Vivienne and Annabelle had no idea how bad things had been. They looked at each other tearfully.

"Go ahead, Martha." Jeremy urged her on. She hesitated, not wanting to continue but knowing she must.

"We arrived in America and Jebediah told us we were to travel on a wagon. I was most unhappy. I didn't like him and the boys didn't like me." Her eyes met Isaac's; he looked away in shame. "In those days many immigrants traveled west searching for a new home. The days were filled with dust, heat and hunger. It took forever to get to Wyoming. Ezekiel was bitten by a rattlesnake and almost died. It was horrible." She stopped to sip her tea. "Isaac can you tell them about Wyoming please."

Isaac hesitated; he turned to Abe who motioned for him to go ahead. "We arrived in Fort Laramie, then we moved to our own land and built a sod house. It was very small. I remember our getting a much larger log home later that year. To be honest, I don't remember much except hunting for buffalo with groups of men. I remember our father was the pastor of the church and we held services every Sunday. Mama is right, I did not like her then nor she me. I was not a very nice boy." Abe patted him on the shoulder and took up the tale.

"Isaac was troubled in those days. Martha tried to be a mother to us but she was young. Isaac was ten, I was eight and Zeke was five. It was very hard for her. Our father beat us often. I remember having a dream about my friend, John. When I woke up, I was scared because I dreamt that he was dead. In the morning, we found out that he died that night. It really frightened me. Father was furious, thinking I was predicting the future. He said he would beat the devil's sight out of me. He dragged me to the shed." Abraham looked to Martha. He was not sure how much to tell. She just nodded. "He beat me with a strap until Mama stopped him. He broke her wrist and locked us both in the shed for two days." Vivienne put her arms around her husband.

"We need to stop now. This is enough. Annabelle, I don't think the children need to hear this." Vivienne was very upset. She had no idea that things had been so bad for them. She rose from her chair. Jeremy told them all to stay where they were; this story was going to be told. Slowly, Vivienne sat back down.

"I told father about the dream." Isaac told the others. "Father asked me to spy on Martha and the others. I didn't know then what I later remembered and I helped him. I am so sorry that I told him, Abe."

"We have been over this many times Isaac, nothing to forgive. It is all in the past." Abe reassured Isaac and then Martha continued.

"Jebediah tricked all of the homesteaders by lending them money. Later he foreclosed and took their farms. He pretended to be a man of God, but he was evil. He stole their land and he did despicable things. Things we can not talk about." She stopped unable to go on. Jeremy picked up the story.

"Martha's father realized what a horrible man Jebediah was and asked Austin Wells and myself to go to America to find them. It took us many months but we finally found the family in Wyoming. We approached Martha but did not let Jebediah know we were there. We wanted Martha to take the boys and leave."

"Let me, Papa." Isaac interrupted. "I was down by the river. I saw Uncle Jeremy and something snapped. I started to remember our real mother and how she died. It all came back like a horrible dream that I had pushed to the back of my mind." Isaac gulped for air. "I could see her at the top of the stairs, I went to find father." Thomas stared at his father. Annabelle held her breath. Sissy sat silently beside her, staring at Isaac. Austin gripped Loretta's hand tightly. She knew something terrible must have happened next.

"Isaac don't." Martha stopped him. She looked at Jeremy pleading him to stop this. Tears poured down her face. She was pale.

"It is time, Martha." Jeremy told Isaac to continue. Isaac nervously gulped for air.

"Abe and Zeke were in the cabin. I found father in the church with Uncle Jeremy. They were arguing. I told father that I remembered how our Mother died. I remembered that I saw him push her down the stairs." Annabelle gasped. *Oh dear God, Isaac. Why didn't you tell me?*

"Isaac that's enough. That is all you need to say." Abe stood up and walked over to his brother. Isaac was breathing heavily.

"No, Papa is right. It is time. I confronted our father, I accused him of killing our Mother." He paused, looking from Martha to Abe, then focused on Annabelle. "I had my rifle in my hand. I shot him dead. I killed my own father."

"Thomas, Sissy, stay here. Isaac come with me." Annabelle took Isaac from the room. He followed trancelike. Everyone else sat frozen in place.

"Jeremy, what have you done?" Martha ran after Isaac. Abe went to Jeremy who looked like he was about to collapse. The strain was too much for all of them. Vivienne held Sissy and Thomas tightly to her.

"I didn't know it was so bad, Auntie Viv. It is all my fault." Vivienne reassured Thomas that none of this was his fault. She held him tight, filled with pain for this family.

"Pa killed that old meanie, I'm glad." Sissy always reduced things to simple terms. Vivienne hugged her close.

Martha found Isaac sobbing in Annabelle's arms. She put her arms around them both. Abraham soon joined them. Annabelle slipped back to her children leaving Martha, Isaac and Abe alone. The three stood and sobbed for several minutes. Martha was taken back to Wyoming, over twenty years before. It was as if they were cleansing their souls of a terrible hurt that was festering for so long. All the pain, all the secrets had been released.

Jeremy waited patiently. It had been a difficult decision but he knew it was time for this secret to end. Vivienne and Annabelle talked to him quietly, reassuring him that the family would survive this. Austin and Loretta stood by, as ever lending support.

"I hope so, I pray to God that I have not done the wrong thing." He looked from one face to the other; all of them closed their eyes in prayer. Sissy came and sat on his knee. At that moment, he missed Anna very much. The thought of Anna made him realize that it was because of her that all of this had come to be. A single tear rolled down his cheek. It also reminded him of the reason for this visit.

"Martha, boys, please come back in and sit down. We have more to discuss." The three returned. Strangely lighter than before. Isaac and Abe even smiled at their wives. It felt good to have no secrets. Thomas ran to his father and Isaac held him tight.

"I ask all of you to forgive me for forcing this, but it was time." Isaac and Abe put their arms around Jeremy. "Martha?" The family looked to Martha and waited. She stood staring at all of them, her face, stained with tears. Jeremy was praying that she would forgive him. She stood for several minutes without moving. Finally, as if a veil was lifted, she continued.

"Jeremy and Austin took us all away from Wyoming after Jebediah died. The townspeople never knew what a monster he was. They loved him and named the town Whittakerville. I don't remember the trip back east, I was just glad that that horrible man was dead. God forgive me for saying that, but life with Jebediah Whittaker was living hell." She paused to catch her breath; her eyes met Isaac's. "Isaac did what was necessary, we never spoke of it again. We came as far as St. Louis and decided to stay here." She looked at Jeremy. Slowly she walked over, put her arm around him and kissed his cheek. "Jeremy and I fell in love, we raised our boys to be fine young men. They married beautiful women and we now have grandchildren whom we love with all of our hearts." Jeremy pulled her into his arms and kissed her.

"Aw, how sweet and they lived happily ever after." Sissy chirped forcing everyone to laugh. The tension was broken, if just for a moment.

"I am very sorry but there is more. Martha please hand me the letter." Jeremy looked at his family, his face held a great sadness. They could not imagine what was coming. He took the crumpled paper and began to read. Austin rested his hand reassuringly on Jeremy's shoulder.

Loretta held Martha's hand. No one knew what to expect but they knew it wasn't good news.

Dear Mr. And Mrs. Whittaker

This letter is to inform you that Anna; your daughter has been arrested for attempted murder. If you want to come to Wyoming to see her before her trial at month end, you must hurry. She will be sentenced to death by hanging if found guilty. I know that you do not feel kindly towards me, however I treated your daughter with the utmost respect and even love. She returned this by trying to poison me. I am sorry to give you such news.

Yours truly,
Jeb Whittaker
Mayor of Whittakerville, Wyoming.

P. S. Mr. Whittaker, I must apologize for hurting you, I was a very angry young man and am a much different person now. Surprisingly I owe it all to Anna.

No one spoke, no one moved. The entire room was silent as if they were frozen in time.

Chapter Thirteen

Family in Crisis

"We have to go to Wyoming, Martha. We have no choice. I must try to save Anna. She can't be guilty of this crime. Jeb must have framed her." Jeremy paced the room.

"What if she is guilty, what then? Oh dear God, what if she is guilty? I can't take this anymore Jeremy. I can't deal with this." Martha started to sob uncontrollably. Jeremy paced faster; he didn't go to her.

"You can't believe she is capable of trying to poison someone, for God's sake Martha, she is our child." After several minutes of silence, he reached a decision.

"That's it. I am going. You can come or you can stay here, but I am going to bring my daughter home." He marched from the room. He was angry and there was no solution to this disagreement. Martha watched him go through her tears. She didn't follow him.

Jeremy left the house and headed for his office. Austin was working late. "I have made a decision, Austin. I am going to Wyoming to bring Anna home." Austin stared at his friend, weighing his words carefully.

"You might not be able to bring her home, if she is sentenced by the court, Jeremy. Do you want me to go with you? You know I will." Austin meant what he said; he would accompany Jeremy to Wyoming, even though he had sworn never to return.

"No, I need you here. I don't know how long I will be gone and the business needs you." Jeremy looked over some papers on his desk.

"Is Martha going with you?" Austin didn't think Martha would be very happy about going back to Wyoming.

"I honestly don't know. Things are strained between us right now." Jeremy looked like he had lost his best friend. Austin's heart went out to him.

"You and Martha can weather this Jeremy, you love each other. It will work out." He wished he had more to say but words failed him.

Out on the farm, a similar conversation was taking place. "I have to do this Annabelle. I swore never to return to that horrible place, but I can't let Papa go alone and I know he will go." Annabelle was beside herself. She didn't want Isaac to leave, but his next statement almost knocked her over. "I think Thomas should come with us. It is time he became a man."

"You can't be serious, he is ten years old. No Isaac, he is not going. He doesn't need to be part of this fiasco with Anna." She piled the dishes in the sink, knocking a glass over. It shattered to pieces. She cut her hand trying to clean it up.

"Leave that, Annabelle. I said leave it. Come here." He pulled her into his arms. "Thomas wants to go. You know how curious he is about Whittakerville, and he is the next generation. Perhaps the town is not to blame for our father's mistakes." She kept shaking her head. "I need him with me Annabelle." She looked up into his eyes. Filled with compassion for the man she loved, she finally nodded in agreement. *Oh dear God, why is this family suffering like this. Anna why did you do this to all of us?*

"What if she is guilty, Annabelle? I know you always see the best in people but Anna is very willful. What if she did try to kill that crazy Indian?" Isaac sat in the living room staring at the portrait of Alicia Whittaker, his mother.

"Isaac, don't even say that. Anna wouldn't kill someone unless he threatened her. Yes, that's it. Jeb. Jr. probably threatened her and she did it in self -defense. Or she did it because he tried to kill Jeremy and this was her first chance to do something about it." Annabelle searched her mind for excuses; she didn't want to believe Anna capable of attempted murder. "But in her letter, she said he was a good man. Oh, I don't know." Annabelle Whittaker didn't want to believe anyone could be so cruel. Isaac was not convinced. "What are you going to do when you get there? I am frightened Isaac, you said you would kill him." Annabelle was shaking. He held her hand tightly.

"I don't know. I don't know what to think or who is guilty anymore. This whole story is so confusing. I did feel hatred toward that crazy Indian, Jeb Jr. as you call him but now I don't know what to think." He ran his fingers through his dark hair. "Somewhere in my mind, I wonder if he was just an angry frightened young man like I was. He saw his mother beaten by the same man that killed my mother. Maybe we have more in common that I thought." Annabelle stared at her husband. She was surprised by this new insight.

"Yes, Isaac perhaps he is a good man after all. I pray we will settle this situation and Anna will come home safely." She closed her eyes as if speaking to God. "You must go and yes, you must take Thomas with you." She pulled him to her, "I love you Isaac." They sat together silently, each in their own thoughts, for a long time.

Abraham and Vivienne arrived a few hours later. They had a similar conversation earlier. "Well what is the final decision, are you going?" Abe looked at his older brother with concern. Isaac nodded. Abe continued, "I have decided that I am not going. My patients need me and someone has to take care of the farm. I know you have all of the crops in, but the animals still need taking care of. Viv has agreed to do that for you and I would not leave without her." Abe didn't have as much trouble making his decision as Isaac did. He wanted nothing to do with Wyoming ever again.

"Thomas and I will go with Papa," Isaac told his brother. Vivienne looked at Annabelle in surprise.

"Thomas? But why are you taking Thomas?" Abraham looked at Viv sternly, trying to quiet her. "What are you thinking, Isaac, he is just a boy. Annabelle, for heaven's sake, do something." Viv was getting very upset. Thomas and Sissy were like her own children and she was very protective.

"We have discussed it, and I agree with Isaac. Thomas is going, come and help me with the tea, Viv." Annabelle ushered Viv firmly from the room. In the kitchen, Viv sank into the wooden chair, tears in her eyes. "Viv what is it? Why are you so upset?"

"Oh, I don't know. I cry at the least thing lately." Annabelle gave her a knowing look.

"Are you with child?" Viv stared at her and then hesitating, nodded her head in the affirmative.

"I think so. Oh, it is a happy time but everything is so awful. Anna is in prison, the men want to go to Wyoming, and Mother Martha is falling apart. I haven't told Abe yet." Annabelle hugged her tightly.

"Well, we need some happy news. Let's go and tell them now." Vivienne hesitated. She didn't think it was the right time. Annabelle felt it was exactly the right time. She grabbed Viv's arm pulling her into the living room. "Viv has an announcement to make, gentlemen." Sissy and Thomas came into the house right at that moment. Viv looked from one to the other.

"Annabelle, the children." Although Vivienne seldom worried about social graces, children were not privy to such matters

"Our children were raised on a farm, Vivienne. You can speak freely in this house." Annabelle nudged her to make her announcement.

"Abraham and I are expecting a baby." A shocked Abe rushed to her side, pulling her into his arms.

"Is it true, we are having a baby?" He kissed her and twirled her around. Sissy and Thomas ran to hug Vivienne. Everyone laughed.

"Be careful of Aunt Viv, now children." Isaac smiled at Annabelle. It was just the kind of news they all needed to cheer them up.

"Congratulations to the new parents." Isaac patted his brother on the back and kissed Vivienne's cheek. "Now you be careful with the farm work, no heavy lifting. Do you hear me?"

"Hey, I'm the doctor in this family. Don't you worry; she will take good care of herself. A father, wow, I can't believe it."

Sissy looked up at Abe in surprise. "What do you mean you can't believe it, you are the Daddy and Aunt Viv is the Mommy, that is how you get babies, silly." Everyone laughed out loud. It was a very happy moment for them all.

"Well, that settles it. I am staying right here." Abe pulled Viv onto his lap in the big armchair. He was very happy. "Nothing is going to spoil this time for us. Isaac, you and Papa can take care of whatever happens in Wyoming." Thomas looked anxiously at his father.

"Don't forget, Thomas. He is coming with me." Isaac looked at Thomas, who ran to him, hugging him tight.

"Oh Pa, thank you. I am going to Wyoming." He was so excited; he nearly knocked Sissy off her feet as he spun around.

"Me, too Pa, I want to come too." Sissy insisted. Annabelle pulled her close.

"I will need you here to take care of the farm, Sissy and Aunt Viv will need you too. You are going to have a little cousin next spring." She looked disappointed but soon forgot all about it and questioned Viv about the baby. Isaac looked at Annabelle with relief. Thomas asked a million questions about the trip. The reason for the trip was almost forgotten in all the preparations and celebrating.

The next day, Abe and Viv went to the Whittaker mansion to tell Martha and Jeremy their news. She was in the conservatory, but Jeremy was not home. “Your Papa spends a great deal of time at the office these days. He is trying to settle everything before he goes west. I just wish he wasn’t going at all.” Martha had large dark circles under her eyes; her face was drawn and pale. Abe was very concerned.

“Mama, sit down. You look ill. Are you feeling all right? This entire Anna situation is taking its toll on you.” He fussed over her. Vivienne watched them from the other side of the room. She was hesitant to tell Martha their news with her mother-in-law looking so distressed. Slowly, she checked the orchids and the ferns bidding her time.

“We have news for you that will make you feel better. Mama, come here Vivienne.” Abraham’s wife moved to his side. “Mama, we are expecting a child.” Martha could not believe her ears. She looked at the two of them.

“A child, that is wonderful. Oh Abraham, thank you for making me happy again. This is just the news we needed. Wait until Jeremy hears this. Oh, Vivienne this is wonderful.” She hugged them both. Her face took on a new uplifted cast; she smiled widely. “Let’s have a party.”

“I don’t think this is the time for a party Mama, maybe when Isaac and Papa get back. Did you know that Thomas is going with them?” Abraham watched her reaction. Vivienne took Martha’s hand and sat beside her on the small settee.

“No, I didn’t know Thomas was going but the boy is fascinated with Whittakerville. He is old enough to go. I wonder if Jeremy knows?” The two young people exchanged a curious glance. Were Martha and Jeremy not talking?

“When will Papa be back?”

"I don't really know. Let's call Charles and have tea to celebrate." Martha seemed hesitant to talk about Jeremy. There was definitely something wrong. Abe offered to find Charles and order the tea. He left the women alone.

In the kitchen, Charles was relaxing with the newspaper. "Charles, Mama would like tea in the conservatory, but before you do that, is there something wrong between them?" Charles looked away, hesitant to discuss personal business. "Charles, please."

Charles looked at Abraham. "Mr. and Mrs. Whittaker are experiencing some difficulties with the Anna situation. I am afraid they have different opinions. Would you like honey with your tea, Sir?" Abraham knew the conversation was over. He was being dismissed. He went to fetch his coat. Abe left the mansion and headed for Jeremy's office.

"I would like you to come home now, Papa. Viv and I have some special news."

"Really son? What is it?" Abraham would rather take Jeremy home but he felt if he made his announcement, he would get more cooperation.

"We are expecting a child. Mama is very pleased and would like you to come home for our celebration." Jeremy picked up his papers, not meeting Abraham's eyes.

"That is wonderful news, Abraham. I am very pleased for you both. I have to finish this before I can leave. I am leaving for Wyoming in two days; we will celebrate when I get back. Please give Vivienne my congratulations." He rose and hugged his son.

Abraham tried again, but it was obvious that Jeremy did not want to go home. Abraham left him at the office and returned to the mansion. This troubled him a great deal; Martha and Jeremy were always able to work through their problems. The more he thought about it, the angrier he became. *Damn you Anna, why is it always you that causes trouble between them? Damn you to Hell.*

Chapter Fourteen

Anna

"Mrs. Whittaker, I can not help you if you don't tell me exactly what happened." The elderly lawyer hobbled across the room. Anna watched him with distaste. She seemed to vacillate between the snobbish aristocrat and the shrew. He placed his briefcase on the table in front of her and plopped into the chair. "Why did you have arsenic in your possession?"

"For heaven sake, how many times do I have to tell you? I use it for my face cream. First you mix arsenic, vinegar and chalk and put it on your face. It gives a nice white glow to the skin. Lot's of women do it back east, I didn't poison anybody." She glared at him. "Now, get me out of here. This place smells."

"I am afraid you are not going anywhere just now, Mrs. Whittaker. Actually, I understand you are not Missus Whittaker but Miss Whittaker. Let me make sure the papers are correct." He shuffled the papers slowly. She grew exasperated with him.

"Can I get another lawyer?" He ignored her. She asked again.

"I am the only one that will take your case. Now shall we begin at the beginning?"

"Send a telegram to Mrs. Esther Hobart Morris, she will find me a proper lawyer." Anna demanded, looking at him pompously, her arms folded in front of her chest.

"Mrs. Morris has informed the court that she has no association with you and that you deserve all you get, in her opinion. I do not think she is a friend any longer. People do not like to associate with felons, my dear." Anna was shocked. What was happening, these important people were her pawns. It suddenly started to sink in. She was in terrible trouble. The lawyer left her alone for a few minutes.

"Get my father, Jeremy Whittaker here. He will straighten this out. That lunatic Jeb Whittaker stabbed my father; he tried to kill him. Are you listening to me?" She screamed through the closed door to no one in particular. "Get Jeremy Whittaker, now!"

The sheriff and Joshua Brown listened to her shrieking from the office. They shook their heads in disgust. Anna had no friends in this town.

"What does she mean, Jeb Whittaker tried to kill her father? Is that true?"

"No, she has been shouting all kinds of ridiculous accusations since we locked her up. She is a lunatic. Filled with pure cussedness, that one. I think we might want the doc to give her something to subdue her." The sheriff had about enough of Anna. "Do I need your permission as her lawyer?"

"Go ahead and call the doctor in, I can't deal with her like this either. I really have no case. She is guilty as sin. There is a witness, the doctor gave a statement that Whittaker exhibited all of the signs of arsenic poisoning, you have the arsenic, so no evidence pointing to her innocence, only to her guilt. Plus one minute she thinks she is Queen Victoria and the next she is screaming like a washer woman." Old Joshua wrote something down and looked up at the sheriff. "You know they are cousins, not man and wife?"

Donald nodded, "Strange situation all around but I like Jeb Whittaker, hell everybody likes him. She will have trouble getting off in this town."

Jeb arrived at that moment. "Donald, Mr. Brown how are you this evening?"

"We would be better if that lunatic woman would be quiet. I am thinking of having Doc give her something to calm her down. Every time I leave her food, she throws it at me. She is a she devil, that one!" Jeb smiled, he remembered finding that quality very attractive not long ago. He frowned, quickly remembering the current situation.

"I was talking to Doc about having her taken to one of the hospitals for lunatics. He said there would be no trouble getting her committed. I don't know what you think about that Mr. Brown?" The lawyer pondered Jeb's suggestion.

"Could do. Might save the court a lot of trouble. I can't even imagine trying to hold a court case, with her like that." Just then Anna screeched through the closed door. The men looked at each other in frustration. "Something has to be done, and soon."

"Well, if you are finished questioning her, I have to put her back in her cell." Donald moved toward the door, he looked over his shoulder at the other two men. "Any volunteers?" The others shook their heads.

The doctor came to see Anna; he managed to slip some laudanum powder into her tea. It seemed to calm her down. The sheriff added it every morning. She wandered around her cell in a trance. She was quiet and that was all the sheriff cared about.

Jeb decided to visit her again before applying to have her committed. In his mind, committing her to an asylum was better than her being hung by the neck until she died. He wanted this all to be a terrible mistake. He wanted his Anna back. The sight of her stunned him. Her hair was disheveled, her face dirty and her clothes hung on her frame. It was obvious that she had lost weight while incarcerated. Anna stared at him blankly. She mumbled incoherently as she walked back and forth in the tiny cell. "Got to get out, got to get out. Can't stay here." Over and over, she repeated those words. Jeb watched her from outside the cell. He was shocked at her appearance. *I loved you Anna, you are no longer the woman that I loved. Why did you do it, why did you try to kill me?* His heart broke to see her like this. He called her name but she did not answer him. He turned on his heel and left the jailhouse.

The trial was to start in three days. Jeb was surprised that he had not had a telegram from the Whittakers. He sat in his office staring out the window. Smithers knocked on the door. "Come in Bill. What can I do for you?"

"Three strangers just got off the train. I think you better come and see them, Jeb. One of them says he is Anna's father." Jeb's head jerked around.

"Anna's father? Jeremy Whittaker is here?" Smithers took Jeb's coat from the rack and handed it to him, nodding in the affirmative. The two men headed for the hotel.

Meanwhile, Anna had a visitor. Alice Parker sat outside the cell talking quietly to Anna. She told her about the children and their lessons and the town's gossip. It was as if she were having tea with a close friend. Anna sat and stared at her blankly, but she did not shriek or throw anything. Donald watched through the opening of the office door with interest.

"Can I bring you some clothes, Anna? The ones you are wearing need to be washed. If you take them off, you can wear this dress I brought you." Alice gestured to the bag lying at Anna's feet. Anna stared at Alice and then at the bag. Moments later, as if a curtain had lifted, she mechanically stood up and started to strip. The sheriff discretely closed the door to the office. Anna carefully folded her clothes, took the dress from the bag and pulled it over her head. She smiled at Alice.

"Hand me those dirty clothes, Anna." Anna passed Alice the bag without hesitation. "I am going to ask the sheriff if I can come and give you a bath and wash your hair. Would you like that?" Anna nodded. Alice passed a book through the bars and said her goodbyes.

Before leaving, she spoke with Sheriff Martin. "She needs a bath and I will be happy to do it. Just be sure she has been medicated and I don't see a problem." The sheriff was impressed with Alice's approach to his prisoner and agreed. When Alice left, Donald instructed his deputy to get a tub and boil some water.

Deciding that Jeb should know how calming Alice was for Anna, he walked toward Jeb's office to tell him about the incident between the two women. He met Bill and Jeb walking toward the hotel.

"Wait up. I have some interesting news about Anna." Donald hurried toward the two men.

"Anna?" Jeb was trying to think of what will happen in the next few minutes when he comes face to face with the Whittakers. "What now?" Donald could see the distress on Jeb's face. He forgot about Anna for the moment.

"What happened? You look like you've seen a ghost."

"Worse my friend, Anna's father is in town." The three men walked slowly to the hotel. Donald and Bill were going to support their friend, no matter what happened.

The doctor gave Anna her laudanum and Alice arrived. A tub was moved into the cell and filled with water by the deputy. Left alone with Alice, Anna cautiously stepped into the tub. She submerged her body into the warm soapy water and leaned back. Alice started to wash her hair. Anna relaxed. She seemed in a trance.

"Help me Alice. Please help me; I can't go into that lunatic asylum. I would rather die." Anna's voice was eerily soft and quiet. Alice stopped and stared at Anna. This was the most coherent she had been in weeks. "Please, I must be free. I heard them talking. You must help me." She paused as if thinking of a solution, "Hold my head under the water."

Alice moved away in fright. The suggestion horrified her. A few minutes later, she moved back. Anna was now silent, staring blankly at the cell walls. Alice continued washing her hair.

Alice finished, dried her off, helped her dress and then sat with her. Alice did not know what to say. Anna begged for her help, but what could she do? Finally she turned to face her, "I don't know how I can help you, Anna." She felt so helpless. Anna was her first real friend.

"Help me kill myself." Anna looked right into Alice's eyes. Again, Alice was shocked.

"No, Anna, no, I can't do that." She looked away.

"Please, bring me some poison or a knife or a gun. I don't want to go to that place where they torture people and lock them up. I can't do it Alice, I can't." Anna was beginning to panic. "I would rather hang." Her actions became jerky. Alice withdrew to the door. The deputy opened it, letting Alice out.

Anna's voice raised, she screamed, "You must help me. You must." Alice hurried out of the jail.

Alice's mind was in turmoil. *Dear God, how can I help her kill herself? I must convince Jeb not to send her to the horrid place.* Alice rushed into her room at the boarding house. The room was small with a dresser, bed, washbasin and several hooks for clothing. The curtains were clean but faded. Several books were piled on a small table in the corner. Everything was well worn but clean and tidy. She sat and stared for hours at the street below her window, contemplating Anna's dilemma.

Meanwhile, Jeb, Donald and Bill arrived at the hotel. "Mr. Jeremy Whittaker's room, please."

"Mr. Whittaker and his traveling companions are in the dining room, Sir."

Jeb turned toward the other two. "Thank you for being here but I have to do this alone. Wait here if you want." He took a deep breath and turned toward the dining room.

Moments later he saw the Whittakers sitting in the back of the room. They appeared deeply involved in a discussion. Their movements were animated hinting that they may be having a disagreement.

Jeb approached cautiously.

"I want to go to the jail right now." Jeremy saw Jeb from the corner of his eye. He jerked around facing him. "You, where is my daughter?"

"Mr. Whittaker, I am sorry to have to see you under these circumstances." Jeb offered his hand. Jeremy ignored it. The others noticed the change in Jeb's appearance.

"Well, you certainly have made some changes. Now where is my daughter, I have no time for small talk." Isaac assessed the new improved Jeb with interest. Seeing that Jeremy had ignored the man's hand, he rose from his chair and offered his hand. Jeb was surprised but took it.

"Jeb, I'm Isaac your half brother. We have come to see Anna." Jeremy stared at Isaac. He could not believe that he was being cordial to this person, possibly the man that had framed Anna or worse. "Thomas, this is Jeb Whittaker, your uncle." Thomas took his father's lead and extended his hand. Jeb shook it with much surprised. Never did he expect Isaac to be so polite. Was that understanding he saw in the face so much like his own? Thomas stared at the two men; the resemblance was uncanny. There was no denying that they were brothers.

"Enough of this, take us to Anna now." Jeremy stood dropping his napkin on the floor. Jeb retrieved it and turned to face his uncle.

"I apologize for my actions in the past. I was a different person then. I can not stress enough how very sorry I am that you were hurt." He looked from Jeremy to

Thomas and then Isaac. " Please accept my apologies. The situation with Anna is a very difficult one. You must be prepared before you see her."

"Never mind, I will find the jail myself." Jeremy pushed passed Jeb, almost knocking him over. Jeb followed him with Isaac and Thomas close behind.

The sheriff saw them coming. "Jeb, do you need any assistance?"

"Sheriff Martin, can you please tell Mr. Jeremy Whittaker about his daughter?" At the sound of the word 'Sheriff' Jeremy stopped. He looked into Donald's face, waiting for an answer. "Mr. Whittaker, please listen to the sheriff. Anna is under a doctor's care." Jeremy jerked around.

"Doctor? What did you do to her, you bastard?"

"Mr. Whittaker, calm yourself. Jeb here did nothing to your daughter. I am afraid she has lost her mind. She tried to kill Jeb with arsenic. Now sit down." Donald led Jeremy to the nearest chair. Jeremy hesitated, but followed. Donald explained the seriousness of Anna's mental state and also the very good case against her. "If you wish to talk to the doctor, I am sure we can find him." In the meantime, Bill Smither's stared at Isaac, trying to remember him as a boy.

Isaac stood watching Jeb. *Are you different? Did we both spend an angry childhood because of that monster? Can you be trusted? You did try to hurt my wife; can I forgive you for that?* He half listened to the sheriff while his mind reeled with his own thoughts.

Thomas could not believe what he was hearing. His aunt had gone mad and tried to kill someone. He watched his father carefully. Thomas was proud of his father. This trip had taught him a great deal about the man.

Jeb was watching Isaac with the same curiosity. Isaac's reaction had surprised him. Never did he expect to be greeted like a member of the family. *The family, this is my family at last. But will you ruin it for me, Anna? Will you be the cause of my losing the only family I ever had?*

Finally, Jeremy was briefed on Anna's condition and readied to go to see her. He entered the jail tenuously. He didn't want to see her behind bars. Soon he stood looking at her. She was asleep on the cot under a thin wool blanket. Asleep, she looked like a little girl, his little girl. His heart was breaking. He wiped the tear from his cheek. She stirred and seeing him she screamed, "Daddy, Daddy, help me. Are you here? Are you really here?"

"Anna, it's me. I am really here. Calm down now. Stop screaming, I am here."

"Get me out of here, they are going to put me in the lunatic asylum. Help me, I want to go home." She screeched. She repeated herself over and over, shaking her head from side to side. He could not believe his ears, she sounded like a madwoman. He reached through the bars to her but she didn't move. She clutched the sheet to her face like a security blanket. Her hair was loose and wild.

"Anna, calm down. I will see what I can do." Jeremy was very distressed. "Go back to sleep." He rushed from the jail. Outside, his stomach retched. His hand reached for the support of the wall, he vomited. Isaac, who was waiting outside, rushed to his aid. Donald Martin pitied Jeremy. *What must the man think? Poor Jeb, what a mess.*

Jeb offered Isaac, Jeremy and Thomas a room in his house, but they declined. Isaac thought is best not to rush into anything with Jeb. He was still a stranger. Isaac didn't completely trust him. Jeb went home where he had a stiff whiskey. Isaac, Jeremy and Thomas returned to the hotel and had a restless night.

Jeremy discussed the case with the doctor and the lawyer. It did not look good for Anna. He went to see her but she was pacing incoherently in the cell and did not recognize him. Her eyes were wild. *Dear God, she looks like my mother. Lost inside of her own head, my child is insane.* Sadly, Jeremy left. He walked the streets of Whittakerville. He didn't know what to do. *Martha I need you here to help me make this decision. Dear God, I have to sign my own daughter into an asylum or watch her hang.* Soon, he found himself outside of Jeb's office; he knocked on the door.

"Come in." Jeb was seated at his desk. He looked up in surprise.

"I need to talk to you." Jeremy took the chair in front of the desk. His shoulders slumped; he looked exhausted. Jeb knew exactly how he felt.

"Whatever you want to know, just ask. Before you say anything, I want you to know one thing. I love your daughter, or I did until she tried to kill me. I think I still love her. I know how hard this decision is." Jeremy looked at him, sizing him up.

"Did she really try to poison you? I want the truth."

"Yes."

"Why, what did you do to her?"

"Nothing, it was about influence. She wanted all the power and the glory. I was just a means to an end for Anna. It wasn't about me; it was about money, power and her total freedom. I didn't want to believe it but, when she was done with me, she tried to get rid of me." Jeb looked away. Jeremy could see the sadness on his face.

"Anna is only a child." His fatherly instincts would not let him believe that this was true.

"No she is a woman; a vindictive, calculating woman that tried to kill me. Now we have to decide what to do with her. She doesn't have a chance to win this case. Her actions are those of a madwoman, she can't just go home." Jeb watched the emotions on Jeremy's face. The same indecision that he himself felt was very apparent. "What is best for Anna? Perhaps one day she could be released from the asylum?"

"I can't watch her hang. I can't." Jeremy was filled with apprehension.

"Can you sign her over to the doctor? I had decided that it was best but now you are here and it is your decision. You are her father, you must decide. I am only her cousin although we lived as man and wife in this town." Jeremy clenched his fist at the mention of Anna as Jeb's wife.

"You took her innocence. You bastard, you stole my baby." Jeremy stood up as if he was going to strike Jeb, but fell back into the chair, defeated. Jeb looked at him with great empathy. After a few minutes, Jeremy stood up; his shoulders slumped in defeat and walked out without a word. Jeb sadly watched him go.

Later that day, both Jeremy and Jeb visited Anna at different times. Joshua Brown reminded them both that the trial was the next morning. The doctor needed a decision. Isaac left Thomas at the hotel and went to see Anna. Alice also paid Anna a visit. Anna begged each and every one of them to help her.

The next morning, Donald Martin returned to the jail. There had been a skirmish during the night and he and the deputy were called away. As usual, the deputy made coffee and prepared a tray for the prisoners. He carried the tray to Anna's cell. It dropped to the floor in a loud clatter.

"Sheriff, come quick!" Donald pushed the door open; the two men froze in horror at the sight that greeted them.

Donald rushed into the cell where Anna Whittaker, lay on her cot. Her bed was covered in blood, her face was almost unrecognizable, and part of the top of her skull was missing. A gun lay on the floor beside her. She was dead. "Get the doctor, hurry up." The deputy ran for the doctor, knowing it was much too late but not knowing what else to do.

Donald Martin stared in shock at Anna's limp body. In her hand was a piece of paper. He pried it from her fingers. Unfolding it, it read. *At last I am free.* Donald stood there aghast.

Jeremy, Jeb and Isaac arrived at the jail after being summoned by the deputy. Donald met them outside. "I am afraid I have some very bad news. Anna is dead."

"Dead?" Jeremy's legs went weak; Isaac and Jeb each grabbed an arm, supporting him.

"What happened to her?" Jeb's voice shook; he could not hold back the tears.

"Shot herself. Someone had to give her a gun and I need to know if it was you Jeb."

"Me, no I was at home. A gun, for God's sake, who would have given a madwoman a gun?" Donald looked at Isaac and Jeremy.

"Don't look at us, we came to save her." The sheriff looked at Jeremy.

"God, what am I going to tell Martha? My Anna, my dear little Anna." He put his head in his hands and sobbed.

"I need to get Papa to the hotel where he can lay down. Do you need us for anything right now?" Donald shook his head. Isaac took Jeremy by the shoulders and walked him toward the hotel. Jeremy walked as if in a trance. Donald and Jeb stared after them.

"Go home Jeb, I'll take care of this." He put his arm around Jeb's shoulders for support. "Come on, I will walk you home." The deputy and the doctor nodded from inside the jail. Everyone was traumatized.

"No, I need to see her. Please Donald, please." Donald moved aside and Jeb walked slowly into the jailhouse. He stared in horror when the doctor pulled the sheet back. "Anna, oh Anna, what have you done?" He collapsed to his knees, head in hands. Donald helped him up. Jeb's whole body was shaking. The doctor placed the sheet back over Anna, looking at Jeb with great pity. Donald guided Jeb toward home.

When they reached the house, the sheriff told Ling Ye and Chu Ying what had happened. They took the two men into the parlor. Chu Ying rested his hand on Jeb's shoulder. Ling Ye brought two stiff whiskeys. After downing the burning liquid, Donald, remembering the note in his pocket, handed it to Jeb. Hands shaking, he read it. Jeb held it in his hand for a long time before he said, "She is finally free, all Anna ever wanted was to be free." He broke down and cried.

The next day, Anna Whittaker's body was placed in a casket for shipping back to St. Louis by rail. Thomas and Isaac went to the church, where years before, Jebediah Whittaker was shot. Isaac paused outside the door. Although there had been additions and changes over the past twenty years, making the building look different, the memories came flooding back. Isaac was frozen to the ground, his feet would not move. Thomas looked into his father's eyes, dark eyes so like his own. He took his father's hand. "Come on Pa, I'll be right here. You have to go in." Isaac looked at his young son with pride. Thomas was quite the young man.

The two of them entered the church, humbly and quietly they approached the altar. It was larger than Isaac remembered. In the front row, on their knees were Jeb and Alice; they turned to watch Isaac and Thomas approach. Thomas guided his father into the pew opposite them. They knelt in prayer. They stayed silent and still for several minutes. Tears rolled down Isaac's face, tears he could not stop. His son also cried, but his tears were for the loss of his auntie and his father's suffering. Thomas loved his father with a deep devotion. Isaac cried for Anna, then he cried for himself. He finally let go of all the guilt that had haunted him for twenty years, with his own son by his side. A new bond was formed that day, a bond of father and son that would never be broken.

The four left the church sometime later. "Please feel free to come to the funeral in St. Louis, Jeb." Isaac looked at Alice and as an afterthought, added. "You too, of course, Miss. Were you a friend of Anna?" Alice nodded, dabbing the tears from her eyes. Isaac felt a deep pity for the plain young woman that seemed so grief stricken. Jeb was surprised by the invitation.

"I would be very pleased to come Isaac. Thank you for being so nice to me. I know I don't deserve it." Jeb was overcome with compassion for Isaac and all of the Whittakers. Alice stood silently staring at the ground.

"Yes, you do. I understand more than you could ever know, Jeb. I suggest you ask God's forgiveness. And then start your life over from this day forward. That is exactly what I intend to do." Thomas smiled at his father. Isaac extended his hand. Jeb shook it firmly. Brothers united in a deep understanding of how the brutality on one man could overshadow and haunt the life of his sons.

"Are you leaving on the train tomorrow?"

"Yes."

"Then I will be on it." Jeb turned to face Alice. "Miss Parker, would you like to join us?"

"Oh, my goodness, Mr. Whittaker. I would very much like to go to Anna's funeral. But of course, I couldn't afford it."

"Not a problem, go and pack a bag. You were Anna's closest friend in Whittakerville. I will pick you up at 8 tomorrow morning." Alice thanked Jeb and Isaac profusely; she shook Thomas' hand and walked quickly away, head down.

"She was very close to Anna, especially at the end." Jeb watched her go. "Alice would have done anything for Anna, anything." Then a curious look crossed his face. Isaac did not miss it. He turned and stared after Alice.

"Do you think she….?" Isaac left the question unfinished. Jeb turned to him.

"I don't know."

A cold, icy blast of air blew through the churchyard, appearing from nowhere, like a blast from the dead. Thomas rubbed his goose bump covered arms. A chill ran down his spine. The three of them turned from the church and headed back into town.

Jeb took Isaac and Thomas around town, introducing them to people and showing them the changes. Isaac barely recognized the town as the same small, pioneer village that he knew. The single street had grown to a small village with side streets and several neighborhoods. He could not help but see the respect and admiration for Jeb in the townsfolk's attitude. His step- brother was a great curiosity to him, but for some reason he felt a very close bond with this man. *And to think, at one time I wanted to kill you, my brother.*

Olga was very pleased to meet Isaac, she remembered him as a sullen quiet boy. Isaac introduced Thomas. Olga stared at them in surprise. The similarity in the three of them was startling. She still wondered where and when Jeb came into the family but she dare not ask. The family was in mourning; it was a terrible shame what had happened in the jail. Olga gave Isaac a letter for Martha, extending her deepest sympathies.

Many of the town's people were shocked when they heard of Anna's suicide. Although some thought she was rather power hungry and ruthless, they never expected her to poison Jeb or to kill herself. The town was shrouded in sadness for Jeb and his family. A small service would be held in the church as a memorial.

Isaac wanted to return to the hotel to check on Jeremy. The doctor had given him something to make him sleep, but he was not handling Anna's death well. Jeb invited Thomas to go to the blacksmith shop and then out in the countryside. Thomas readily accepted. He wanted to see as much of Whittakerville as he could before the train departed tomorrow. Thomas and Jeb rode out onto the plains, Jeb pointed out a herd of Prong-horned antelope. Thomas had never seen such creatures. An hour later, Jeb found what he had been searching for. "Look Thomas, bison." Thomas stared at the huge herd of bison grazing in the meadow. Large brown heads swayed back and forth, a large bull raised his head in their direction. The bull turned back toward the herd, then suddenly dropped to the ground. He began gyrating to and fro, creating a huge cloud of dust.

"What's he doing?" Thomas was fascinated.

"That big fellow is trying to attract the females. The larger the dust cloud, the more impressed they will be." Jeb pointed out how the females seemed to be watching the bull. "Look's like he has a few takers." Thomas laughed. He was thrilled with the sights and sounds of the plains. The distraction was welcome. Jeb enjoyed showing Thomas the beautiful countryside and the creatures that lived there. He was pleased that Isaac trusted him enough to allow Thomas and he to ride out alone. It spoke volumes to Jeb.

Jeremy lay on the bed in the hotel; his head was groggy from the medication. Tears ran down his face, his breathing was shallow. *Dear God, please take care of my Anna. She was a troubled soul and I loved her with all of my heart. Such terrible choices for the end of a young life; I just couldn't imagine her in that lunatic asylum. It would have killed her. But, never could I have stood by and watched her hanged. My dearest daughter, I know deep in my heart, that this was the best result for you. Anna please forgive me for failing you. God forgive me.* He sobbed uncontrollably.

Isaac returned to the hotel and checked in on Jeremy. He knocked, then opened the door. Jeremy was awake. Isaac took the only chair in the room. "Are you alright now, Papa?" Jeremy nodded. The two discussed how the rest of the family was going to react when they found out about Anna. Jeremy had no idea how to tell Martha, he decided not send a telegram. Isaac had not sent one to Annabelle either, they would just go home and tell everyone in person. It was going to be a very long trip back to St. Louis. Isaac's heart went out to Jeremy, he could see how much he was suffering.

The next morning, the casket was loaded on the train but Anna Whittaker's spirit remained in Wyoming. Jeremy, Isaac, Jeb, Alice and Thomas boarded at precisely 9 a.m. The whistle sounded, the train slowly chugged away from Whittakerville. Isaac went to the platform at the back of the caboose; he stood and watched Whittakerville and his past disappear in the distance. *Goodbye Father, for once and for all, you are dead and buried. You will never haunt us again. Goodbye Anna, God forgive you.* A single tear rolled down his cheek. He didn't see Jeb standing back in the shadows; he too was saying goodbye to the only woman he had ever loved.

Chapter Fifteen

A Family in Mourning

The funeral was to be held at 3 p.m. Loretta made all of the arrangements with Hans Kruger's assistance. Hans was very upset when he learned of Anna's death. He had loved her and once thought they would have a life together. Dozens of large bouquets were placed around the room, the oak casket sat on the pedestal surrounded by floral beauty. Lilies, roses, daisies, chrysanthemums and flowers of all color and shape filled the room with a rich floral scent. A portrait of Anna stood on a stand beside the closed casket. The walls were shrouded in deep burgundy velvet. Several chairs were placed around the room. It was the most distinguished funeral home in St. Louis and no expense was spared.

"Hans, can you make sure the caterer knows what time to serve the food? I spoke with him earlier but I don't want anything to go wrong. Poor Martha and Jeremy are under enough stress, you and I must be sure everything is in order." Hans smiled at her.

"Don't worry, you have done an excellent job. Mrs. Whittaker will be very satisfied. I will go now." Hans picked up his overcoat from the chair. He glanced sadly at the portrait and left the room.

Loretta double- checked once more. She was very worried about Martha and wanted to stop in before going home. Loretta stopped in front of the casket. "*Well Anna, you got your wish. No rules, only total freedom, where you are now. God forgive me for thinking this but your family will be better off without you. Even in your passing you have caused my son David great pain, almost destroyed your parent's marriage and filled our lives with misery.*

Goodbye Anna Whittaker, may God forgive you. Loretta turned and walked out of the room. Moments later, the portrait of Anna toppled mysteriously to the floor as if bumped by an invisible hand. The frame shattered with a loud crash.

At the mansion, Martha lay motionless on the bed. Vivienne and Annabelle took turns sitting with her but she didn't say a word. She wouldn't eat and they forced her to take sips of water. The women were very worried. She had been like this since she was told about Anna' death, three days earlier. They told Loretta that there was no improvement, when she arrived.

"Martha, it's Loretta. Come on now, you have to get up and choose your gown for the funeral. Life goes on Martha; you have children and grandchildren that need you. Jeremy needs you." Martha didn't move; her eyes stayed focused on some far away object. Loretta tried again. "Martha, now enough is enough. You can't do this. We have a business to run. Anna is gone, you can't bring her back." Still nothing. Loretta was frustrated; she went to find Annabelle.

Martha lay motionless. Her mind was blank, her heart broken but no tears fell. Her daughter was dead. It was all her fault. Martha wanted to die.

" Maybe one of the boys can reach her. This is most disturbing; I know she thinks it is all her fault. What are we going to do?"

"Let Sissy talk to her." Vivienne surprised both of the others with this statement.

"Sissy? Dear Lord, I am trying to spare the children. How can Sissy possibly help?" Annabelle had explained Anna's death as best she could to her children. She wanted to spare them as much pain as possible.

"Please Annabelle, let me take Sissy in to see Mother Martha, what have we got to lose?"

Vivienne was very convincing and Annabelle called for Charles to bring Sissy into the parlor. “Yes Mama, Charles said you needed me?”

Vivienne took Sissy by the hand. “Sissy, Aunt Viv and Mama have a very big job for you, a most important job. Grandma is very, very sad because of Aunt Anna’s death. We would like you to go and talk to Grandma.” Sissy looked at Vivienne with large eyes.

“Okay, I will go now.” She skipped from the room and ran up the stairs before the adults could stop her.

“Let her go Annabelle, see if it works.” The three women watched Sissy disappear and waited impatiently.

Slowly Sissy opened the door to Martha’s room. She walked over to the large canopy bed and climbed up beside Martha. Without saying a word, Sissy cuddled into Martha, kissing her cheek. After a few minutes, Sissy gently wiped a tear from her grandmother’s cheek. Martha turned her head to look at Sissy. She pulled the tiny girl into her arms and started to sob uncontrollably. Sissy held her tight. The two lay together for almost an hour. Finally Sissy spoke, “Grandma, I know that you are very sad. I know you are going to miss Auntie Anna very much but I will be here with you. I want you to know that I love you. You are the best Grandma ever.”

Martha looked at her tiny granddaughter. A narrow smile on her lips, she kissed Sissy’s head. “Grandma loves you too Sissy. Grandma loves you with all her heart. Thank you, my darling Sissy.” She hugged Sissy tightly. Sissy slipped off the bed, kissing Martha’s cheek.

“I will be right back, Grandma.” Martha again stared at the ceiling. The cry had helped her feel alive again. *How will I get through the funeral? How can a mother bury her child? I did love you, Anna, I did love you.* She wiped the tears as they fell. Her body felt heavy. *I must, I must do it for Sissy and for the rest of the family. I must be strong.* Moments later she sat up, weakly throwing her legs over the side of the bed. She sat there until Loretta came in.

"Martha, are you feeling better?" Loretta sat beside Martha, putting her arms around her.

"I was just thinking about how my own father was instrumental in bringing in the Lunacy Act in England, so many years ago. He had visited Jebediah and Jeremy's mother in the asylum and he was so distraught at the conditions, he dedicated himself to improving things. Anna's grandmother was insane. Anna's uncle was insane and dear God, Anna was insane." Loretta pulled Martha into her arms.

"Martha, don't."

"I have to accept it Loretta. It is the only way I can accept the knowledge that my daughter killed herself." Loretta held Martha, her heart breaking for her friend.

"Abby is so far away, I miss her terribly but I can't imagine how you feel knowing you will never see Anna again. Martha. I am here for you." Martha looked into Loretta's face, and hugged her tight. The door squeaked as Sissy entered the room. Loretta kissed Martha and left the two of them alone.

"Grandma, you are awake. Good, Mama says we have to be strong. Mama says we have to pray for Auntie Anna. Pray with me Grandma." Sissy knelt beside Martha's bed. Martha sank to her knees beside Sissy. Together they prayed. Martha kissed the top of Sissy's red head.

"Come on, Sissy, there is much to do. We must make Auntie Anna's farewell the best it can be. We must let her know that we loved her very, very much and that we will miss her." Sissy jumped up and took Martha's hand. Martha washed her face and fixed her hair. Together they ascended the huge staircase, much to the surprise of Annabelle, Loretta and Vivienne. Vivienne smiled at Sissy. *I knew you could do it Sissy, my little angel.*

Jeremy stood in his office staring out of the window. “Drink this Jeremy, you are going to need your strength.” Austin handed Jeremy a large brandy. Jeremy took it unconsciously, draining the contents in one gulp. “Loretta said the arrangements are all made and we are to be at the funeral home by 3 p.m. I brought your suit from the house, you can change here and we will go.”

“Thank you Austin. I can’t get the sight of her out of my mind. The last time I saw her, my darling Anna. She had this wild- eyed stare that looked right through you. She screeched like a banshee one minute and then paced frantically back and forth the next. She begged me to help her die. My own child begged me to help her commit suicide.” He collapsed into his large leather chair. His head in his hands he sobbed. Austin put his hand on Jeremy’s shoulder.

“Let it out man, I know how much you loved her. I don’t know what I would do if anything happened to Abby.” Austin didn’t know what to say or do. He just let Jeremy talk.

“She wanted me to give her a gun. How could she beg her own father to help her end her life? You can’t imagine the state she was in Austin, it was horrific.”

“Don’t talk about it now, Jeremy. Come, get dressed, we must be going. I am sure the memories will haunt you for a long time, but right now we must get to Anna’s funeral. Martha will be waiting for you.” Jeremy stood and walked as if in a trance toward his dressing room. Austin watched his friend with great sympathy. He didn’t know how to ease his pain.

Isaac met Abraham at the hospital after his rounds. “You can’t imagine what she looked like Abe. It wasn’t the same Anna.”

“Anna, dead. I have trouble believing it. Almost as much trouble as I am having with your newfound love and understanding for Jeb.” The two men left the hospital.

"Jeb is okay, Abe. We don't know what terrible things happened to him when he was growing up. What happened here in St. Louis was just the result of our father's hatred and treatment of his mother. I understand him."

Abraham climbed into the wagon beside Isaac. "You were going to kill him."

Isaac took the reins, holding the horses at bay. "I know, but I was wrong. Just give him a chance; he really is a good man. The people of Whittakerville hold him in great regard and he loved Anna. Even after she tried to kill him, he still loved her."

"Well, I will give him the benefit of the doubt, if you say so. If you can go full circle, so can I. When are we supposed to be at the funeral home?"

"Annabelle said 3 p.m. She and Viv will meet us there. God, this is horrible, burying our sister at such a young age. I just hope Mama and Papa can survive this. It is tearing them apart."

"Ezekiel and Abby sent an telegram. There is no way they can be here from England but he is as concerned as we are about Mama and Papa."

"Let's go, we'll be late." Isaac jerked the reins and the horses began to move.

" By the way, how did Thomas like Wyoming?"

"Thomas made me very proud, he has grown into a fine young man. I don't know what I would have done without him in Wyoming. You can ask him yourself once we get this funeral over and done with."

Jeb and Alice Parker arrived at the funeral home by carriage, from the hotel in St. Louis. Alice, wearing a plain black dress and bonnet, walked into the room first. She stopped and stared at the broken portrait on the floor. Jeb rushed over and picked it up. He pushed the frame back in place and set the portrait on the stand. Splinters of wood hung from the bottom and sides of the frame. He stared at

Anna's face with such sadness. Alice watched him from the other side of the room. *She is gone Jeb, it is what she wanted. Anna is gone.*

Alice moved to the side of the room and took her seat. The chairs were arranged in rows and a large podium sat at the front of the room. More people arrived, taking their seats. Agatha Carruthers, Arthur Langley, May, Ellen and Frank Borman and many others attended. Several people whispered about the man in the front of the room. Jeb remained at the casket. Isaac and Abraham entered the room. They moved to Jeb. "Jeb, this is Abraham." Abraham shook hands with Jeb and then looked at Anna's portrait.

"What happened to this?" He fingered the splintered wood.

"I'm not sure, it was on the floor when Miss Parker and I arrived. I fixed it the best I could and put it back on the stand."

"Ghosts?" The three looked at each other and moved to take their seats. Abraham sat in the front row. Jeb was heading for the back but Isaac gestured to the seat beside him. Abraham nodded and feeling rather uncomfortable, Jeb sat down. Soon Thomas, Sissy and Annabelle, carrying Amy, arrived. They sat beside Isaac. Sissy stared at Jeb. Finally she could not contain herself and leaned towards him. "Hi, my Pa said you are sorry for being so bad. He said you are not that crazy Indian anymore. I'm glad." Annabelle was horrified. Jeb stared at her, he didn't know what to say.

"That's right, Sissy, now shush." Isaac grinned at Jeb. Jeb relaxed a little.

Vivienne took her place beside Abraham but not before staring at Jeb. She leaned into Abe, "Is that who I think it is? He looks a lot different than last time I saw him." Abe nodded and took her hand. Vivienne leaned forward catching Annabelle's eye; they exchanged a look of apprehension. To them this was still the man that had attacked them. It would be difficult to forget that.

Martha and Jeremy arrived with Loretta and Austin, proceeding quietly to the front. Martha's hat was the latest style, an inverted flowerpot in black. The hat was much smaller than previous fashion. A veil covered her face. Her gown was a black silk taffeta, two piece with a ruched bodice and pleated cuffs and hem. They sat in the front row staring straight ahead at Anna's casket. Loretta held her hand. No one spoke. When Jeb had replaced the portrait, it was repositioned so that Anna's eyes stared out into the room, seemingly staring at all of them. It was very disconcerting to everyone.

Hans Kruger took the seat in the back row next to Alice. She nodded to him shyly. Hans introduced himself. "I understand you were Anna's very good friend in Wyoming." Alice nodded, twisting her handkerchief nervously in her hands.

"I was engaged to Anna before she left St. Louis. I loved her. Thank you for being her friend, I am sure she appreciated you very much." Alice blushed.

The reverend proceeded to the podium and the service began. The organ played solemnly in the background. Tears flowed freely, as they all said goodbye to one so young.

The burial took place in the cemetery of the church where Abraham and Vivienne were married. Everyone was uncomfortable, remembering what had happened there. A cold wind blew, leaves twirled in the air like ghostly birds. Black clouds covered the sky. Jeb, did not want to be there. As soon as the casket was lowered, he walked away. Alice was about to follow him but was intercepted by Hans, who offered her his carriage to the reception. She watched Jeb go, turned and accepted the invitation from this very handsome young man. She felt comfortable telling him about Anna, how she had bathed her in the jail and taken care of her. She told him how terrible it was to see Anna so distressed. Alice told Hans how Anna had tried to kill Jeb with arsenic, using Anna's tumultuous mental state as an excuse. Hans listened attentively. In the back of his mind he was thinking about the close call he had. *I almost married Anna, then it might have been me that she tried to poison. Thank you, God for my broken heart.*

Everyone filed away from the mound of earth that was now Anna Whittaker's resting place. Rain began to fall. Jeb returned to the grave. His tears mixed with raindrops, sobs came from deep within. Alone he said his goodbye, placing one single red rose on the earth. *I will always love you, Anna.* His hand reached for the ring hanging around his neck on a gold chain. He clutched it tightly in his fist. A cold chill ran down his spine, he felt so alone.

At the reception, Vivienne and Annabelle stood together at the side of the buffet table. "I just can't relax around Jeb, Abraham and Isaac seem so accepting of him all of a sudden. He makes me nervous," Annabelle whispered before chasing after Amy. Vivienne nodded. She watched Jeb from across the room. Martha approached with Sissy close behind.

"Have you eaten anything, Mother Martha?"

"No, Vivienne, I have no appetite. It was a lovely service, wasn't it?"

"Yes, Loretta and Hans did an excellent job. Thank God for Loretta. What do you think of Jeb?" Martha followed Vivienne's glance.

"Isaac explained to us that Jeb has changed. He also said that Anna was responsible for that. It is good to know that Anna did something memorable and worthy before she died." Martha could tell that her daughter-in-law was not convinced.

"Just give him a chance, he will be gone in a few days. It seems to be very important to Isaac and after his confession; I don't want anything to upset him. He is finally at peace." Martha seemed to look at nothing in particular and then added, "So is my Anna, did you know that she left a note that read: *At last I am free*. How strange, I said those same words when Jebediah died." Martha wandered away in a trancelike state.

Dear God, what did this family endure in Wyoming? Vivienne took a bite of the cookie that she had been holding; her appetite was insatiable.

Abraham smiled as Thomas described the bison, the antelope and the wilds of Wyoming. Even he had to admit, that as a child, he too had been very impressed with the nature and the beauty of the countryside. Abraham was surprised to learn that Isaac had allowed Thomas and Jeb to go alone into the plains. *Perhaps some good did come from this trip to Whittakerville. I have not had a pleasant thought of Wyoming in years.* Abe told Thomas some stories of his childhood in Wyoming, pleasant stories. It made him feel much better about Wyoming.

Jeremy had not spoken to Jeb, but found himself standing beside the young man. "I just wanted to say, I am sorry for being so rude to you, young man. Isaac has made me realize that you did not harm Anna, in fact just the opposite. You told me that you loved Anna and I believe you." He extended his hand to Jeb. Jeb looked into Jeremy's eyes. He gripped his hand; tears welled up in his own eyes.

"Yes, we both loved Anna and we both will miss her. But she is free at last." With that he walked out of the house. Jeremy watched him go. Martha came to Jeremy.

"What were you talking to Jeb about, Jeremy? It looked very serious."

"He loved our daughter, everything else is to be forgotten where Jeb is concerned. He loved Anna with all his heart." A strange look came over Jeremy's face. "Can you say the same, Martha?" Jeremy turned and walked away from her. She stood very still. Not realizing she was holding her breath, she felt suddenly faint. Her knees started to buckle. Abraham caught her just in time. "Mother, what is it? Do you need to lie down?" Martha looked at her son.

"Your Papa hates me Abraham. He hates me." She began to sob uncontrollably and Abe signaled for Loretta to take her upstairs. Abraham went to Jeremy.

"What did you do to Mama, she just told me that you hate her. This has gone too far. You love Mama and she loves you, Anna is still causing trouble even in death. Go to her this minute. She is in mourning, she needs you."

"She doesn't need me. She didn't love Anna the way I did. I don't know if she loved her at all." Jeremy turned and left the house, leaving Abraham shocked and silent.

The next few days saw Jeb return to Wyoming with Alice. Isaac and his family tried to get back to a normal life. The only thing different on the farm was that Sissy was staying in town with Martha. Sissy would not leave Martha's side and everyone agreed that she seemed to be the best medicine for Martha. Jeremy stayed at the office, sleeping in the small flat in back. Abraham went to the hospital, Vivienne helped Isaac on the farm and life went on.

"Grandma, I think you should go to the dress shop. Auntie Loretta must be very busy there. I will come with you." Sissy paraded around Martha's bedroom wearing one of Martha's hats. She looked very comical in the oversized hat with the ostrich feathers. Martha laughed at her.

"Sissy, you are absolutely right. How did you get so smart for someone so young?" Martha was overjoyed that Sissy was staying with her. She was a wonderful distraction and kept Martha from thinking about Jeremy, who had been gone for over a week.

"Broccoli and carrots."

"Broccoli and carrots? What on earth do you mean?"

"Mama said that if you eat all your broccoli and carrots, you'll be smart. They taste disgusting but looks like they work." Martha laughed out loud. She hugged Sissy close, knocking the hat from her head.

"Okay, Miss Smarty pants, let's go to the shop." Together they finished dressing. Martha dressed in a simple black, dulled taffeta skirt, long sleeved black blouse, fitting for a woman in mourning. Before she left the house, she placed a small hat with veil on her head and headed into town. Martha felt better than she had since learning of Anna's death.

"Sissy, Grandma wants to stop at Granddad's office but I will take you into the shop first." The carriage stopped and Sissy climbed down.

"Okay Grandma, I will help Auntie Loretta until you get there." Sissy skipped off into the dress shop, the bell on the door tinkled loudly as she entered. Loretta looked up and smiled. "Grandma is going to see Granddad, she will be here soon. Now give me some work to do. I want to help." The child's words were like a wonderful news flash to Loretta. *Perhaps they will work out their differences. Bless you, Sissy.*

Martha held her breath; her hand shook as she reached for the doorknob. She closed her eyes and prayed, *Dear Lord, help me say the right thing. I love Jeremy with all of my heart. I need him. Please Lord, be with me.* She opened the door. Jeremy looked up in surprise when he saw her standing there. He was unshaven and without his suit jacket.

"Martha."

"Jeremy, I'm so sorry." Her voice trembled. She stood just inside the door afraid to come any closer. "I love you Jeremy. I loved Anna. I really did." He stood and walked to her side. “Please Jeremy, I need you.” He reached for her and pulled her into his arms.

“I know you did. I’m so sorry Martha. I love you.” Together they cried for their lost child, holding each other tenderly.

All of the Whittakers dealt with their grief in their own way, but it was a sad time for all of them.

Chapter Sixteen

Understanding

"Let me take Amy home with me, just until tomorrow. I need to start practicing being a mother." Vivienne jostled baby Amy on her knee. The child soon grew fidgety, wanting down. Carefully Vivienne placed her on the floor and the little one waddled away. "She is walking very well, Annabelle. Besides, with Sissy gone and Thomas at his friend's, you and Isaac deserve some time alone." Vivienne was trying to get this family back on its feet. She wanted to see them smile again.

"You really don't have to do that Viv." Then as an afterthought she added, "But if you want too, why not?" Annabelle packed a small bag for Amy and Vivienne beamed from ear to ear. "Isaac and I have not been alone since Thomas was a baby. It would be nice to have him all to myself." Viv left in the wagon with an anxious Annabelle waving goodbye.

"Why is Viv taking Amy?" Isaac strolled from the barn, his long legs taking large strides toward her.

"Viv thinks we need some time alone, what do you think?"

"I think I love Vivienne, come here my wife." Isaac pulled Annabelle into his arms. At five feet she barely reached his chest but she snuggled close. "What shall we do with ourselves?"

She smiled pulling her apron over her head. "We shall think of something." She led him coquettishly, into the house. He followed anxiously.

"Abraham, I'm home and I have a surprise." Vivienne carried Amy into the warm cozy kitchen. A large pot of soup was cooking on the stove, Abraham appeared from the living room. "My goodness, supper on the stove. What a wonderful husband I have. Look who's here." Amy gurgled at Abraham, reaching for him with chubby arms.

"Amy, my little sweetheart. What's the occasion?"

"I thought Isaac and Annabelle needed some alone time. And, you need to start practicing, so Amy needs her diaper changed, Daddy- to- be." Abraham laughed, kissing Viv quickly on the cheek.

"Diapers are no challenge for Uncle Abe, come on Amy." Amy giggled as Abe tickled her. Vivienne smiled at the two of them. *What a beautiful sight. You will be a wonderful father, my love.*

"Abraham, what do you really think of Jeb?"

"Isaac convinced me to give the man a chance and that is what I am doing. You should do the same." Abraham tossed Amy's soiled diaper into a bucket and lifted the toddler into the air.

"He almost killed me. It is a little difficult to forget that." Viv took the bucket to the backroom, where she filled it with water from the pump.

"Yes, I know. However, he didn't kill you and that was when I realized that I loved you and could never lose you, so actually you owe him a debt of thanks." Abe snuggled Amy, she giggled. Viv returned to the living room.

"A debt of thanks! That is stretching it a bit. No, I don't think I can go that far."

"Just try and forgive and forget. He lives in Wyoming for heaven's sake, we probably will never see him again." Amy wriggled in his arms. "Here, practice being a mommy for awhile, I will serve supper." Vivienne took Amy. She was having trouble with Abraham's solution of forgive and forget. Vivienne was not that forgiving.

Later that night, Vivienne lay awake listening to Abraham sleep. His even breathing was soothing to her ears. She was remembering the men that killed her father. Dressed as a boy, she had hunted them down and shot them. It was so long ago but she could still remember the satisfaction when she knew they were dead. *An eye for an eye, that is how I was raised.* She looked at Abraham. The bright moonlight shone in the window, giving the room a soft glow. *For you my love, I will try. For you and our beautiful child that is growing inside of me.* She patted her belly gently and fell fast asleep.

That night Abraham tossed and turned. He dreamt of his father. Jebediah Whittaker stood in the Wyoming churchyard. He laughed an evil laugh; his eyes glowed like burning coal. Suddenly, Anna appeared in the dream, she stood beside Jebediah laughing the same sinister, evil laugh. Jebediah stared at Abraham laughing, "I have won, at last. I have won." Abraham screamed. Vivienne woke suddenly, finding her husband sitting up in bed, a look of horror on his face. *So, you do not forget that easily my love.* She put her arms around him.

Isaac and Annabelle ate a delicious dinner and then retired for the night. The time together had been good for them. "Isaac, can I ask you about Jeb? I really am trying to accept him as your brother, but I can't get the memory of what he did to me out of my head." Isaac sat up in bed, pulling Annabelle into his arms.

"Jeb was a very troubled young man. I understand it. I want to tell you about Wyoming, about when I was a boy."

"No Isaac, I know how painful that is for you, I will adjust."

"Annabelle, no more secrets. It actually feels good to be able to talk about it. Going back to Whittakerville was like lifting a curtain; a curtain of guilt and hidden memories that needed to be lifted. I guess I can thank Anna for that."

"Yes Isaac, thank Anna. I know you will miss her. I also know you didn't always like your sister. It would be good to place a thankfulness upon her memory." Annabelle wanted Anna to rest in peace. She wanted Isaac to come to terms with her death.

"Thank you, Anna, may you rest in peace. Dear God, take our Anna to your bosom. Amen." He opened his eyes; Annabelle smiled at her husband. She knew he was humoring her, but she felt it was the right thing just the same. "Now, about Whittakerville. When we went to the church, I honestly said goodbye to all the hurt and pain. As a young boy, I had blocked out the memory of my mother's death. I was angry and quiet and I didn't know why. I was actually the closest to my father because I was his spy, his accomplice, if you will. I held on to a lot of guilt when I finally remembered that it was him that had killed her. I went insane at that moment, and I shot him. I am just thankful that I came out of that nightmare. Anna was not so lucky."

"How does that have anything to do with Jeb?"

"Jeb was mistreated all of his life as a boy, his mother was beaten and used as Jebediah's sex squaw. When she died, Jeb transferred all of his hate onto his father and this family. That is why he came here to destroy us. Jeb was living in hate and hate can do terrible things to a person's mind. I honestly believe that he went a little insane when he stabbed Papa. The man I met in Whittakerville was completely different. He was a man who knew love. Love is a powerful medicine, Annabelle." She watched his face; she knew he was feeling comfortable talking about this. Annabelle snuggled close and remained silent. "Jeb found love with Anna. He found respect and yes; love, from the people of Whittakerville. I experienced the same kind of transformation after my father was shot. Martha and Jeremy loved me with all their hearts. I was horrible to Mama before he died and it didn't matter, she still loved me." Annabelle watched Isaac's face when he spoke of Martha. That family had endured so much and yet the love they had for one another was unbreakable.

"Anna did that for Jeb, although it appears she didn't really love him at all. I am beginning to understand, Isaac." Annabelle realized that Isaac had pushed many emotions into the recesses of his mind for many years. She felt that this was a healing process for him.

"That's true, poor Jeb was fooled into thinking that Anna loved him. I don't honestly think Anna ever loved anyone."

"Isaac, please don't. You have asked God to accept Anna, leave it at that, remember her fondly." Isaac kissed the top of her head. She always wanted to do what was right and gracious. He loved her with all his heart.

"I have no doubts that my wife and my children love me and that is very important to me, Annabelle. I might not tell you enough that I love you, but please never doubt it."

"I won't Isaac, and I will forgive Jeb for his past sins. I will go to church on Sunday and ask the Lord to forgive him. From now on, I will think of him with kind loving thoughts, of course, we may never see him again." She closed her eyes, "Good night, my love."

"Good night."

Martha and Jeremy returned to their busy schedules. The Haute Couture and the export business were very busy but every evening, they made time for each other. Both of them were determined to close this gap that had developed in their relationship.

"How are things at the dress shop, Martha?"

"Wonderful, we just got a huge custom fit order from California. We have several customers in the east but this is a real breakthrough in the west. Hans came up with the idea of a catalogue of our designs and it has been a huge success. Of course, ready-to-wear is not really our niche, but high fashion is a necessity in the upper classes, even in California. Rail travel has helped immensely making the shipping of the garments much quicker."

"Yes, I must say it was far quicker and more pleasant traveling to Wyoming by train than it was the first time around. The Union Pacific is comfortable and fast. I remember taking different stagecoaches and riding horseback through the dust bowl. The train is clean, quick and efficient. You would not believe how the towns have grown along the rail lines. I was telling Austin that we must start taking advantage of it. There are many open markets out west." He put his newspaper down and picked up his brandy. He swirled the amber liquid in the glass, staring at it as if it were a crystal ball.

"What was Whittakerville like, Jeremy? I have this letter from Olga. I was so surprised that she was still alive. I must write to her right away."

"Whittakerville is much bigger than when you lived there. It has several large stores, even a dress shop now. The train station is a hub of commerce. There is a huge sawmill outside of town, several banks, a couple of saloons, a jail and a courthouse." At the mention of the jail, sadness descended over Jeremy's face. Martha reached for his hand.

"Don't think about it Jeremy. We have buried our daughter and we have prayed for her soul. Let her rest in peace. We will miss her for the rest of our lives but we can't bring her back. Let her go." She looked into his eyes. He knew she was right but a single tear rolled down his cheek.

"Yes, you are right we have been over this subject enough. We must let her rest in peace. I wonder how poor Jeb is handling this whole affair. He really did make a full circle in his attitude as well as his appearance. He thanks Anna for that. He loved her, Martha. I could see it in his eyes."

"Yes, I think he did. He must be grief stricken poor man. I realize now that what he did to this family, was not his fault." Martha shuddered at the thought; "Jebediah Whittaker took another victim before he died. Isaac and Jeb suffered the most, the oldest and the youngest sons of that monster, had to live through the hate that he sowed." Jeremy kissed the back of her hand. "I said a prayer for Jeb. It is time for this family to move forward."

"Yes, my darling. It is time."

Back in Wyoming, Jeb wandered the empty house. He was lonely. He missed Anna. His grief was slowly passing but everywhere he looked, he saw her. He heard strange creaking noises at night, sounds of footsteps on the stairs as if she were still there. He spent time with Donald and Bill and the other men at the saloon, but when he came home, the loneliness returned. He was a young man with needs. He visited one of the saloon girls but that did not satisfy him. It was love he sought, not sex.

Alice visited him often, but Alice was not Anna. Alice was quiet, and kind. She was not vibrant, and full of life as Anna had been. Always planning, scheming to make life better and more exciting, that was his Anna. He even missed the new closeness with Isaac and the Whittakers. Ling Ye and Chu Ying were fussing over their newborn baby boy. Jeb assured them that they would have a place with him for many years. He went to work each day but being the mayor didn't have the same importance. He still wore the ring that he had given Anna on a chain around his neck. Weeks passed but nothing seemed to matter anymore.

One morning, a letter arrived from St. Louis.

Dear Jeb:

I want you to know that all of us have forgiven and forgotten what was in the past. We consider you a member of this family. All of us know and understand how you suffered at the hands of Jebediah Whittaker for we also, were his victims. You loved Anna. You are our link to her. If you feel inclined to visit, please do not hesitate. Our doors are always open to you. I trust you are working through your grief and your great loss, although she may not have said so, I am sure Anna loved you in her own way. She was a very troubled girl who in her own words is "Free at Last." Find solace in that, as I have done.

Please keep in touch,

Sincerely,

Martha Whittaker.

He could not believe that the matriarch of the Whittaker family had written to him. He was very touched by her words. He folded the letter and placed it in his desk, he would always keep it. *Perhaps you are right Mrs. Whittaker, perhaps in her own way, Anna did love me and I loved her enough for the both of us.*

Chapter Seventeen

David

"Mother, are you here?" The tall handsome young man in the naval uniform drew several glances from young ladies passing by the Haute couture. Hans looked up from his work, as the bell tinkled.

"May I help you?"

"Hans, my goodness, it has been a long time."

"David, why I hardly recognize you. You look very smart in that uniform. How is the navy treating you?" David walked around the show room fingering the fine fabrics of the gowns as he passed. He was much taller than Hans remembered him and much more mature. "Your mother will be thrilled to see you."

"Is she here?"

"No, she and Mrs. Whittaker have gone to Chicago on business for a few days. They will be back tomorrow." David looked disappointed but soon brightened.

"I guess it is just the old man and me then. I will go and see my father. Hans, nice to see you again." The two young men shook hands and just before David walked out the door, Hans added. "My deepest sympathies in Anna's death. I know you and she were very good friends since childhood." David stopped and turned to face Hans.

"I should not tell her fiancé this, but I loved Anna more than life itself. It nearly destroyed me when I heard that she had taken her own life. I came back to get the entire story, letters can be very sparse."

"I am sure the Whittakers and your family will fill in the details. Anna and I were engaged for a short time, however, she left St. Louis with another man and lived with him as his wife. Apparently, he is the one that she tried to kill. I look at it as a close escape myself."

"Well, I don't believe any of that. Anna would never try to kill anyone; I am surprised to hear you say that. Didn't you love Anna?" David was disturbed by the comment.

"I thought I did, but it appears you were much more in love with her than I. I apologize if my comment insulted you. Perhaps we will have lunch before you return to your ship."

"Perhaps." David turned and left the shop. Hans watched him go.

David walked across the street toward the export business. The sun felt good on his face. Austin and Jeremy were discussing a trip west to make new contacts. The window was open to allow the cool breeze in. Both men stood with shirtsleeves rolled up in the heat of the day. The door opened and both turned to see who it was. "David, dear God, is it really you? Why didn't you tell us you were coming?"

Austin ran to his son and embraced him. Holding him at arm's length, he looked him up and down. "Looks like you have grown a foot and gained twenty pounds. The navy is feeding you well, I see."

"Father, great to see you. Yes, the navy takes very good care of me. Uncle Jeremy, nice to see you again. I am very sorry about Anna." David and Jeremy exchanged a look of understanding. These were the two men that loved her unconditionally.

"David, you have grown into a fine young man. That uniform is very becoming." Jeremy wiped the sweat from his brow. "Although you must be warm in this heat. I am sure all of the young ladies in St. Louis will be knocking on your door before you leave town. You mother and Martha will be back tomorrow."

"Let's the three of us go for dinner at the hotel. Just we men, oh, it is good to have you back, Son. With Abby in England, the house seems so empty. Grandma Minnie will be thrilled to see you." Austin was ecstatic. His son, the boy, had come home a man.

The men enjoyed a long delicious dinner at the hotel. Ceiling fans kept the diners cool as they sipped cool drinks. "This weather is wonderful for this time of year, perhaps we won't see snow until after Christmas." After a wonderful visit, Austin took David home to see his grandmother. She was thrilled. She asked him all about the ship, the places he had seen and the men that he worked with.

"Last year the Navy Secretary requested funds from Congress for the construction of modern ships. The request was rejected but this year they finally authorized the construction of three steel cruisers. I am hoping to be assigned to one of them."

"Where will they be used, David?" Austin wondered how far away his son would travel.

"Interest is increasing in Samoa and Central America, Father. There is a canal building scheme in the works and of course, other countries have been building up their navies and we must be ready."

"The USS Chicago is the largest of the three ships, and the one I hope to be on. By the way, I had a lovely visit with Abby and Ezekiel when I was in England."

"Your mother and I were in England some time ago as well. Abby seems very happy."

"I went there to visit the British arms establishments with Commodore Simpson. We visited the Royal Arsenal at Woolwich and the Elswich Works at Newcastle on Tyne. That is when I spent two days with Abby, after which we traveled to seven steel manufacturing plants that made ingots and steel masses for casting cannons. All of this was in aid of our country establishing a Naval Gun Factory.

Most interesting assignment." Austin was very impressed with his son's newfound knowledge. David had grown up a great deal since running off to join the navy.

"What did you think of Pheasant Run?"

"Oh, I was truly impressed, it is a most imposing country home. Abby seems to fit the role of 'Mistress of the Manor' very well. She took me to see your family home as well, Grandma."

"Your mother was very upset when Abby left for England. We missed her terribly. You missed a lovely wedding." Minnie added, placing a plate of freshly baked cookies on the table.

"Grandma, I have missed these cookies almost as much as I missed you." He picked one up, savoring the flavor in his mouth before swallowing. "You haven't lost your knack, Grandma. Delicious and oatmeal, my favorite, did you know I was coming?"

"No, but I make them all the time. I knew one of these days you would be here to eat them. Welcome home, David. I have missed you." She placed a kiss on the top of his head and excused herself to lie down. Minnie was not as young as she used to be.

"Is Grandma alright?" David watched his grandmother, who shuffled from the room.

"Yes, Son, she is just getting old. Her arthritis bothers her more and more and she has slowed down a great deal. But she still makes the best cookies in town." Austin reached over, taking two cookies from the plate.

"David, why did you do it?" Austin popped half a cookie into his mouth.

"Why did I do what?"

"Why did you say that you were the father of Anna's child and then leave town? We know that wasn't the truth. Can you please explain to me, what you were thinking? We were very hurt and upset."

"I'm sorry for causing you any pain. Anna asked me to help her and I could not refuse. I loved Anna. I can't explain why I did it or even how I felt about Anna. I just had to help her; there was no other choice. She was my friend and I loved her. I am going to miss her very much." His voice started to tremble. Austin put his hand on David's shoulder.

"Alright son, enough. I will not speak ill of the dead, but Anna was not as innocent and needy as you thought. Your mother sees her as a conniving, liar that ran off with the man that stabbed her father. Whether she planned it or not, no one will ever know. But she used him and then tried to kill him. Jeremy says she was totally insane before she killed herself."

"I can't believe it, Anna insane. Dear God, what could have driven her to it?"

"I just want you to know that your mother holds Anna responsible for your leaving. She had no sympathy where Anna was concerned. I don't want you to be upset when she comes home. I am not sure what she will say. Try to understand, your mother loves you and Abby more than anything."

"I know Father, it is fine. I realize that you both love Abby and me very much. I will miss Anna. I always dreamed of marrying her. I came home to hear the truth, but perhaps that is not what I really want."

"Jeremy will be happy to discuss it with you however, he is rather biased as far as Anna is concerned. Isaac might be a better choice."

"Oh, speaking of biased, I saw Hans today. He said something rather strange. Intimated that he considered himself lucky that he didn't marry Anna, or it might have been him that she tried to kill. I am afraid I just don't believe that Anna tried to kill someone without good reason." Austin could see that David was in denial. The subject turned to other things. Father and son enjoyed the rest of the evening. It was good to be back home. David was very sad about losing Anna, but happy to be home with his family again.

In another part of town, Abraham visited Jeremy before going home. "David is home on leave. Austin is thrilled," Jeremy stated before asking Charles to bring them a brandy.

"Mother will be happy to see David. She was always very fond of him." Abraham looked at Jeremy, he thought better than to mention what Anna had done to David. How she had used him and then not given him another thought. Jeremy seemed to sense what Abraham was thinking.

"I know what you are thinking. Anna was very cavalier where David was concerned. She knew he would do whatever she told him to and she used him. I will not excuse her behavior but let's talk of something else. How is your wife feeling?"

"Vivienne grows larger everyday and is feeling wonderful. She spends as much time with Amy as she can. 'Practice' she calls it." Jeremy laughed.

"Martha and I are looking forward to being grandparents again. Sissy has been a Godsend to Martha. That little girl is old beyond her years. I am sure Annabelle is happy to have her back on the farm but I miss the little imp. It was fun having her here to greet me when I finished work." Abraham chatted for a few more minutes and then headed home. He was happy to see things improve between Jeremy and Martha. They were very important to all of the Whittaker boys. Abraham wanted everyone to be happy. He didn't like discord. He stopped at Isaac's farm on his way and let them know that David was home. Isaac would want to see David before he left town again.

"Hello Sissy. I just talked to Granddad and he is missing you." Sissy carried a large basket of eggs into the kitchen. Annabelle took the eggs and poured Abe a coffee.

"I miss him and Grandma too, they spoiled me. I like it at their house."

"Yes, they did spoil her. Now I have to retrain her all over again." Annabelle laughed. "Please go and tidy up your room, Sissy." Sissy moaned and headed for the stairs, her red pigtails bouncing as she walked.

"Oh Mama, make sure you don't tell Uncle Abe the secret." Sissy put her finger to her lips signaling Annabelle to keep quiet.

"Secret, what secret?" Abraham looked from Sissy to Annabelle.

"Sissy Whittaker, you go and clean your room right now. There will be no telling of secrets, do you hear me?" Annabelle shook her finger at Sissy, who disappeared up the stairs.

"I hope we have a little girl just like Sissy." Abe sipped at the hot coffee, enjoying the fragrant aroma between sips.

"Be careful what you wish for. She can be a handful. I am sure you will be happy with either a boy or a girl." Abe nodded.

"I assume you are not going to tell me the secret?" Annabelle ignored him. "I just stopped by to let Isaac know that David is home for a few days."

"David! Oh that is wonderful, Loretta will be thrilled. She really misses her children." Annabelle folded laundry as she chatted. Abraham finished his coffee and headed home.

He admired his large farmhouse as he rode between the tall poplars that lined the drive. Viv had done wonders with the property and it looked more inviting every time he came home. He was not good with gardens or repairs but his wife certainly was. She had planted wild flowers along the path giving the house a very welcoming appearance. He was very proud of her.

Vivienne rushed out to meet him. “Darling, you’re home. There is a problem in the drive shed, can you come and look?”

“Oh, Viv can’t it wait? I’m tired and I just want to put my feet up and relax. I will look at it tomorrow.” Vivienne gave him a stern look.

“No, you will look at it right now. I take very good care of the maintenance around here, but this time I need you to look at something and you are going to help me.” She gave him her best pout. He pulled her close.

“Oh, alright show me this big problem. I shall get my trusty hammer and smash something to pieces. You know how good I am with tools.” She laughed out loud. “And then maybe I can have my dinner.” Vivienne took his hand and led him towards the drive shed at the back of the house.

As the large door opened, light from the setting sun filtered into the dark building. Particles of dust floated in the air. Abraham stepped inside just as a small squeak could be heard from the corner. Abraham looked at Vivienne with curiosity. “Perhaps we have rats.”

“You go over there and check, I don’t mind most things but I do not like rats.” She stood her ground. Abraham walked toward the corner where the noise could be heard, his eyes slowly adjusting to the dim light. As he approached, straw rustled, suddenly a small brown puppy, bounded toward him. Surprised, he knelt down and the puppy licked his face. Abraham was overcome with joy.

“Vivienne, who is this? He looks exactly like Bo.” Abraham lifted the boisterous bundle into his arms. The puppy continued to lick his face. Abraham laughed and laughed. Vivienne smiled widely. She could see the joy on her husband’s face, just the result she was looking for.

“His name is Little Bo and you can bring him into the house now. Aren’t you glad that I made you come and see the drive shed?”

"Vivienne, I love you and I love this little bundle. How can I thank you?"

"You can get your tools out and put that shelf back up tomorrow." She laughed, put her arm in his and walked toward the house. Little Bo wriggled and squirmed in Abraham's arms. Abraham was a very happy man.

The next morning Isaac rode into town to see David. They went for breakfast at the hotel. "I can't believe that Anna went insane, Isaac. Something terrible must have happened to her. Why was she in Wyoming anyway?"

Isaac had known David since he was born. He knew that David loved Anna all of his life and so he chose his words carefully. "David, a lot has happened since you have been gone. I am going to tell you from the beginning, please let me finish before you interrupt me. I understand that you are not going to like some of what I tell you, but please try and take it in, before you dismiss it." Isaac looked at David, waiting for him to agree before going on. David moved the eggs around on his plate before responding.

"I understand Isaac, I know what you are about to say will not be pleasant."

"A man came from Wyoming to stalk our family. He had his reasons, which I will not go into now. Let me just say, that there was an inheritance involved and he thought that we Whittaker men stood between him and his money. While he was in St. Louis, he attacked my wife, almost killed Abraham's wife, Vivienne and then stabbed my Papa. All of us were in the church office when he came in. Abraham and Vivienne were just married and about to sign the registry. This man came in, grabbed Papa and held a knife to his throat. He ordered all of the Whittaker men to kneel before him and fully intended to kill all of us. Somehow, your father and Anna talked him into letting us sign a letter that would get him his inheritance. Anna then told him she would go with him. We were all shocked. No one knew if Anna knew this man or was being a heroine. Of course, we wanted to think the best of her. Long story short, he stabbed Papa and he and Anna ran from the church. We couldn't catch them because all of the horses were gone. Later, we learned that someone visited Mama and Papa's mansion, stole clothing and money from the safe. It was not a break-in. This led us the believe that Anna may have been in on this plan."

"Anna would never plan to kill or maim her father. She just wouldn't do it. And besides wasn't she engaged to Hans?" David could not help himself; Isaac knew that he would interrupt.

"Let me finish. They disappeared and although we had the police searching for them, they were not found. The horse that they rode away on was Thomas' Chestnut and it returned to our farm several days later. It was several weeks before a letter arrived from Anna. In the letter she said that she was with Jeb, he is the man that stabbed Papa, and that he was not a bad man. She was happy and did not wish to be found. Of course, Papa and Mama were devastated. We didn't hear anything for months and months, until a letter arrived from this man Jeb, saying that Anna was in jail for trying to kill him and that she would be hanged if found guilty. Papa, Thomas and I went to Whittakerville, Wyoming. When we arrived, Anna was in jail but not the same Anna that we knew. This Anna was quite insane. I saw her for myself David; she had lost her mind. She even begged Papa for a gun so she could end her life. Of course, he didn't give her one. But someone did. Before we could make arrangements to have her committed to an asylum, she shot herself in the head." David gasped, tears rolled down his cheeks.

"Anna, my darling Anna. Why? How could this happen?"

"I am afraid our family has a history of insanity. My grandmother was in an asylum in England for years, my father was definitely insane and now it appears Anna inherited that sickness. It is very sad."

"What of this man, did you find him and have him arrested?"

"No, actually Anna was right about him. He really is a good man, with a very sad history that made him do some terrible things, but our family has forgiven him. You see; he is my stepbrother. We never knew he existed. He loved Anna with a great devotion, like you, David. This man truly loved Anna, we suspect he was the father of the child that she lost." At the mention of the child, David's head jerked up.

"You mean she knew this man then, when she talked me into saying it was me!"

"Yes, David. I am afraid Anna used you as she used Jeb and then tried to kill him. You must believe me, David, I am sorry to disillusion you where Anna is concerned but she was not a nice person. Perhaps it was the sickness." David was beside himself. The girl that he grew up adoring could not be this person that Isaac described.

"It can't be true Isaac, it just can't."

"I am afraid it is, David. It is time for all of us to forgive Anna; she is with God now. Let her go and move on with your life." David wiped his face with his handkerchief and stood up. He straightened his uniform jacket, picked up his cap and snapped to attention. Isaac stood also. David extended his hand to Isaac, thanked him and turned stiff backed, and walked away. Isaac sat back down and finished his coffee. This had taken a toll on him but his sympathy was with the young man that just left. *You will meet someone special one day David, a woman that will love you. Anna loved no one but herself.*

Isaac stopped to see Jeremy before going home. "How is David? I am sure Loretta is 'over the moon' having him back home." Jeremy picked up his jacket from the chair. "It was nice of you to take him to breakfast,

Isaac. I am going to work at home today, you can walk with me."

"I enjoyed seeing him again, he has grown into a fine young man. I tried to help him get over Anna's death as best I could. He loved her very much."

"I wish you could help me get over it, Isaac. I feel so guilty every day of my life."

"Guilty? Why do you feel guilty, you had nothing to do with Anna's sickness or her suicide." Isaac held the door for Jeremy.

"I feel like I let her down. I should have been a better father. I could have done something different." Jeremy carried his jacket as they strolled.

"No, don't do this to yourself. You were the best father that girl could ever want. If anything you spoiled her. Do not beat yourself up over this. She was sick, she had mental problems and she killed herself. That is no one's fault." Isaac walked to the mansion with Jeremy, trying to talk sense into him.

"Isaac, how wonderful. Good afternoon, Darling." Martha kissed Isaac and then Jeremy. "I will have Charles bring us a cool drink in the parlor." Jeremy placed his coat in the closet and headed for the parlor, leaving Martha and Isaac alone.

"No really, Mama, I must get back to the farm, we have hay bales to bring in. See if you can talk to Papa about Anna, but only happy memories. He is having a very hard time. I know you are too, but he needs you now."

"Yes, happy memories are what all of us need. Vivienne told me that Abraham has been having horrible dreams. Did you know that she got a puppy for Abraham? It's a surprise."

"I wondered if you had anything to do with that. Remember how Abe brought Bo home to you and said it was your birthday present? You had no choice but to let him keep the dog." Isaac laughed, remembering how

Abraham had fooled Martha so long ago. Martha smiled at the wonderful memory.

"Vivienne asked me about some of the happy times and I mentioned that story to her. She immediately decided a dog was just what Abraham needed to cheer him up. I hope this will help him get over Anna's death. We all grieve in our own way." She looked toward the parlor. "All of us need cheering up. I will go and talk to Papa. Thank you, Isaac. I love you." Martha reached up and kissed her son's cheek. Isaac smiled at her, turning toward the door. His thoughts were a reflection of Martha's, *yes, we all must think of happy times and look forward, not back.*

Martha poured the cool lemonade, and sat beside her husband smiling. "Remember the time Anna slid down the banister and almost knocked poor Pastor Richardson to the floor?" Jeremy looked at her and started to laugh. The two of them laughed until tears rolled down their faces. Many funny stories were told that afternoon, laughter filled the Whittaker house once again.

Loretta and David strolled along the cobbled street, arm in arm. She glanced at this young man that her child had become, with pride. They approached the stone arch that led to the cemetery. She turned to him. "Are you sure you want to do this, David?"

"Yes, Mother. It is time to say goodbye. Thank you for coming with me." Slowly they entered the hallowed ground. Flowers dotted several of the head stones; an old woman tended the grave of her husband. She smiled at them as they passed.

"Here it is David, would you like some time alone?" David nodded and Loretta moved towards the end of the line of stones giving him some time with Anna. He stared at the headstone. It was large. An angel in flight perched atop the rectangular marble, under the angel were the words "Free at Last." His eyes moved downward to read, Anna

Lillian Whittaker, beloved daughter of Martha and Jeremy. Tears filled his eyes; he reached for his handkerchief.

Loretta watched her son; her heart was breaking for him. After a few minutes, she moved toward him placing her hand on his arm. He turned, putting his arms around her. Together they cried.

"David, I am glad you brought me here. I am afraid I did not think fondly of Anna. I blamed her for driving you away." She dabbed her face with her handkerchief.

"Mother, please. You must forgive Anna, she was ill. I know that now."

"Yes, David, I am sorry. I realize now that she was not responsible. I beg her to forgive me. I beg God's forgiveness as well." Loretta knelt at the foot of Anna's grave, pink rose petals, browning at the edges, covered the ground. She sent a silent prayer skyward. David said his own goodbye to his best friend.

As they turned to leave, a mourning dove cooed in the tree. In unison, they said, "Goodbye, Anna Whittaker." Later that day, David left St. Louis, to return to his ship.

Chapter Eighteen

A Surprise

The family settled into their routines. Isaac tended to his farm; the harvest was good that year. Abraham's list of patients grew, as did Vivienne's figure. He teased her often; she loved the idea of being pregnant and anxiously awaited the birth of their child.

Just after Christmas, Minnie Wells passed away in her sleep. This time it was Martha that planned the funeral for her grieving friends. Everyone would miss Minnie very much. Neither, David or Abby was present at the funeral. Martha and Jeremy supported their friends, as they had always done. The past year had tested them all but the bonds of friendship would not be broken.

Just as the buds appeared on the fruit trees, Edward Jeremy Whittaker was born. He was a chubby, happy baby and his parents were very proud. Little Bo, who was not so little anymore, slept beside the cradle, guarding the newest member of the Whittaker family.

On a bright and sunny summer's day, Vivienne sat on Martha's front porch watching baby Eddie sleep. Little Bo lay sleeping beside the chair. Martha was due home any minute and Viv was enjoying the day. She rocked her baby gently, the heat of the day making her sleepy. Little Bo's low growl alerted her. Suddenly she realized a man was standing in front of her, she jumped. "Please, don't be frightened. I am sorry I startled you."

Vivienne regained her composure, squinting at the gentleman before her. Shocked, she didn't know what to say. The dog continued to growl, he moved between Vivienne and the man. Her stomach was in knots; she swallowed the bile that crept up her throat. Finally she found her voice.

"Jeb, what are you doing here?"

"Hello, Vivienne, I have come to see Mrs. Whittaker. Is she home?"

Vivienne held the baby close to her chest. She wanted to run. The dog continued to growl, his eyes focused on Jeb. Sensing her nervousness, and wanting to put some distance between himself and the dog, Jeb backed down the stairs.

Jeb motioned to the baby. "Who is this?" Nervously, Vivienne pulled Eddie's blanket back to show his face.

"This is Edward Whittaker." Then as an afterthought, she added, "Your nephew." Now Jeb was the one that was shocked. Not to learn that Vivienne had a new baby, but that she would refer to him as the child's uncle. He was very pleased and the smile on his face could not hide what he was feeling. Vivienne moved to the door, calling to Charles.

"Charles, please take Edward up to the nursery." Handing the small babe over to Charles, the butler looked passed her at Jeb.

"Is there a problem, Mrs. Whittaker?"

"No Charles, everything is fine, please take Edward inside." Vivienne wanted her child away from danger; it was all she could think about. "Little Bo, come here." The dog moved to her side. His growling ceased but his eyes remained fixed on Jeb. Once the door closed, she took a deep breath and her courage came back. She turned to face Jeb.

"So, you are back. Well, before you see anyone else in this family, I have something to say." Vivienne put her hands on her hips, taking a defiant stance. Jeb was confused. A moment ago she seemed almost friendly.

"Please Mrs. Whittaker, I am not here to harm you or your child. I owe you a huge apology."

"Yes, you do. You dragged me from my horse and beat me within an inch of my life. I do not think a simple apology is going to fix that." She leaned toward him, the words formed with a clenched jaw. She was very angry; her whole body shook.

"I am so sorry." Jeb clutched his hat in his hands; she was making him very uncomfortable.

"Sorry doesn't cut it, mister!" She leaned close to his face, invading his space. Now Jeb was getting his own temper up.

"Hold on a minute, you shot me. I wanted revenge." Jeb stood taller, trying to justify his actions.

"Shot you! I shot you because you were dragging Annabelle into the woods, or have you forgotten that?" Jeb recoiled at her words.

"No, I have not forgotten. I was a different person then. A man filled with hate and rage." Jeb lowered his eyes in shame. Vivienne began to falter.

"Well, maybe so but I am not like the rest of this family. I do not forgive and forget so easily. I want you to remember what I say to you. Never forget these words." Jeb raised his head, looking her straight in the eyes. He waited.

"If you ever hurt a member of this family again, I will kill you. Do you hear me? I said, I will kill you." She repeated the words firmly and slowly. "I mean every word of it. Do I make myself perfectly clear?" Vivienne stared into his eyes, defiantly. He knew she meant every word.

"I understand Mrs. Whittaker. Again, I cannot apologize enough for what I did to Mr. Whittaker. I am surprised that the rest of the family is so forgiving. I do not deserve it."

"No, in my opinion, you don't; you are going to have to prove yourself to me, I am not that gullible. The

Whittakers are fine, God-fearing people who want to see the best in everyone. They are my family now and I will die protecting them. Do I make myself clear?" In spite of the threats she was making, Jeb liked Vivienne's spunkiness, her defiance reminded him of Anna.

"Yes, very clear. The Whittakers are also my family now. I have wanted a family all of my life, it is all I ever did want and I am not going to do or say anything to mess it up. I understand how you feel, but you will see. I will show you that I am a different person." He pushed the lock of dark hair from his eyes. "Anna showed me how to love, for the first time since my mother died. Anna taught me how to talk, how to dress and how to control my temper. She remade me into a new person, a better person." At the mention of Anna's name, Vivienne decided that she had made her point. She would keep a very close eye on Jeb. He could feel her relaxing. "Please, accept my humble apologies and let's try to get along. Can we start over?"

"Alright, I am going to give you the benefit of the doubt. But don't forget, I will be watching you. Don't mess up." Vivienne extended her hand. She was shocked when Jeb, bowed and kissed the back of it.

"Mrs. Whittaker, how lovely to see you again." He released her hand, and smiled at her.

"Mr. Whittaker, nice to see you again. Would you like some tea?" She curtsied, and in spite of herself, she giggled. Jeb laughed out loud.

"If you call off your guard dog, I would like to sit." Vivienne told Little Bo to move and Jeb walked up on the porch. He stood beside one of the large wicker chairs.

"Now, tell me about my nephew. Edward did you say his name was?"

"Edward, after my father, he is two months old. Abraham and Isaac will be pleased that you have come." She motioned for him to take the seat beside her. Little Bo settled between them. They waited for Martha to come home. Conversation was polite and grew more relaxed as the time passed.

Martha arrived an hour later. “Vivienne, how lovely to see you. How is my little grandson today?” She looked for Eddie before she realized that Jeb was there. She froze.

“Hello Mrs. Whittaker.” It took a moment for her to regain her composure.

“Jeb, what a surprise.” Martha sensed the relaxed atmosphere between Vivienne and Jeb; she was relieved. “Both of you come inside.” Martha opened the door and they entered the foyer. “Charles, please bring us some tea. We have a guest.” Martha pointed to the parlor and Vivienne and Jeb followed her.

Vivienne excused herself so that she could check on the baby. Jeb looked at Martha nervously. “I am sure you wonder what I am doing here.”

“Actually, if I remember correctly, I told you that you would always be welcome in our home, Jeb. How are things in Wyoming?” Jeb relaxed at Martha’s easy- going attitude. Charles appeared with the tea.

“Things are lonely. I miss Anna very much.” Martha could tell that Jeb was sincere, she felt very sorry for him.

“Yes, we miss her as well. How long will you be in town?”

“I thought I would visit with Isaac and Abraham and perhaps discuss some business with Mr. Whittaker. The railroad has a new distribution warehouse in Whittakerville and I thought he might be interested in doing some exporting to the west. It was actually Anna, that arranged the deal with the railroad.” His eyes took on a faraway look, before he added. “I was ill at the time.”

Martha knew that Jeb’s illness was the result of Anna poisoning him, but did not comment. Obviously he didn’t want to discuss it. “How interesting, I never thought of Anna as a business woman.” Martha had never seen this side of Anna, perhaps Jeb could tell her more. "What other things did Anna do in Whittakerville?"

"She organized a suffragette movement, she also helped to organize the prohibition movement in Whittakerville. Anna was very proactive in town politics." It appeared that Jeb was bragging about Anna. Martha was very surprised at this entire conversation. "Alice Parker owed her job to Anna, she was very grateful. She was one of Anna's dearest friends." Martha began to feel that she had never known the woman that her daughter had become. She was grateful that Jeb was here to tell her about Anna. She asked him more questions and found his descriptions of Anna's life very interesting.

Jeremy arrived home and Vivienne, holding Eddie, met him in the foyer. "We have a visitor." Jeremy gave her a quizzical look. "It's Jeb." Jeremy was surprised. He kissed the top of Eddie's head, smiling at the little bundle. Composing himself, he and Vivienne entered the parlor.

"Why Jeb, how nice to see you." Jeremy offered his hand and Jeb stood up, accepting it. The two men smiled. "Martha, isn't this a nice surprise?" Jeremy looked at Martha not knowing how she was reacting to Jeb's visit, however she seemed very relaxed. He took his cue from her.

"Jeb was just telling me about Anna's business deals in Whittakerville, it seems our daughter was quite the business woman." Jeremy, surprised, turned to Jeb.

"Actually, I came to see you Mr. Whittaker. As I told Mrs. Whittaker, the railroad has built a depot and warehouse in Whittakerville and I thought perhaps you might be interested in exporting to the west." Jeremy was surprised for the second time.

"It is funny you mention it, because Austin Wells and I were just talking about a trip west to investigate possibilities there. But first, please call us Jeremy and Martha, we are your family, after all." Jeb was overcome with joy. He sat, staring silently at the family before him. Jeremy and Martha, Vivienne with little Eddie and tears rolled down his cheeks. Embarrassed, he quickly wiped them away, but not before Martha and Jeremy saw them.

"Let's get the family together for a family dinner. Vivienne can you go to the hospital and get Abraham? Leave Eddie with me. I will send one of the servants to Isaac's farm. This is a wonderful excuse for a party." Martha rose and started her preparations. Jeb started to protest.

"Don't worry about it, Jeb, Martha looks for any excuse to have a party. You might as well get used to it. Come on; let's leave the women to their chores. You and I can have a game of billiards and a nice cigar before the entire clan arrives." Jeb followed Jeremy, never in his life had he felt so welcome.

Vivienne stared after him, her eyes fixed on the back of his head. He could not believe this reception but suddenly, in the back of his mind, Vivienne's warning rang loud and clear, "I will kill you." He knew she meant it. He turned and saw her watching him. Vivienne made sure he saw her before she walked away. He remembered how Anna had tried to kill him, he shuttered as a cold chill ran down his spine. He pushed the thought away, following Jeremy to the Billiard room. *This is my family at last; I will not do anything to destroy that, thank you Anna.* His heart filled with love at the thought of Anna, in spite of everything that had happened. He still loved her. His hand moved to the ring around his neck.

Several hours later the entire Whittaker family gathered for an evening meal. The long dining room table was filled with fragrant meats. Chicken, beef and pork, accompanied by vegetables of all description sat on plates near to overflowing. The candle flames danced in the slight breeze from the open window. Wine glasses sparkled as the family took their seats. Jeb was given the place of honor next to Jeremy. It was the chair that Anna had occupied for years. Before beginning, everyone bowed his or her head in prayer.

Vivienne's eyes never left Jeb, who was seated directly across from her. Abraham noticed his wife's obsessive stare and tried to distract her. She looked at him but was soon staring at Jeb once again. *What is this all about my love?* Abe would get to the bottom of it after the meal. Everyone was in good spirits. A toast was made to the Whittaker family and to welcome Jeb into their home. Jeb was humbled by the gesture. Other than Vivienne's constant surveillance, he was enjoying himself immensely.

Plates were passed, and appetites satisfied. Between the main course and dessert, Sissy finally could hold back no longer. "Pa, what am I supposed to call Red Fox? You said he wasn't 'that crazy Indian' but you didn't tell us what to call him." Isaac looked at Sissy, who was seated between him and Jeb.

"I apologize Sissy, you can call him Uncle Jeb, if he doesn't mind, of course." Isaac turned and looked at Jeb.

Jeb smiled widely. "Uncle Jeb, it is. I am honored to have such a wonderful niece and a wonderful family. Thank you all for your generosity of spirit." He raised his glass to Jeremy and then to Martha seated at the other end of the long table. Sissy leaned toward him.

"Okay, Uncle Jeb are you going to come and visit us on the farm. You remember those silly ducks that I was chasing when I met you? Well, they had babies and I want to show them to you. Is that Okay, Pa?" Isaac nodded. It was as if any discomfort had dissolved in an instance.

Everyone started to talk at once. Jeb asked Isaac about the farm. Jeremy and Abraham were discussing the new wing at the hospital. Annabelle asked Vivienne how she was feeling. Martha sat back smiling. *What a wonderful family party. Jeb is fitting in very well. Thank you God.*

Anna we miss you, but you are here through Jeb. I think he knew you better than any of us.

Jeremy looked down the table at Martha. She was beaming with delight; it made him very happy to see her smiling. She looked up and he winked at her. Abraham looked from one to the other. The love between them was strong; they had survived. Abraham offered a silent prayer of thanks.

Later as the family strolled in the garden or gathered around the piano, Jeb was feeling a happiness he had never felt. Martha played for everyone, songs were sung and the room was filled with merriment. Jeb thanked Martha and Jeremy many times during the evening. Martha discussed Anna with him. She truly wanted to know the Anna that Jeb had known. Jeb watched Vivienne chatting with Annabelle and Martha from across the room. *What a beautiful woman you are, and so full of life. Just like my Anna.*

Abraham and Isaac returned from the patio. The attention that Jeb was paying to Vivienne did not go unnoticed. Abraham tensed. Isaac looked at his brother. "Don't misunderstand his intentions. He knows Vivienne is your wife. He is just admiring her beauty." Abraham made a fist. "You should feel flattered, now, go and talk with Jeb." Isaac gave Abraham a gently push in Jeb's direction.

"Abe, lovely night. I am truly enjoying this family. Your wife is lovely, if I may be so bold." Jeb didn't want any misunderstandings and he had seen Abraham's face from across the room.

"Yes, my wife is lovely, thank you." Abe was sure to emphasize 'my wife.' "Papa tells me that you are here to discuss the possibility of shipping goods west. He is very excited about it." Abraham drew a breath and relaxed. He could tell that Jeb did not want any trouble but he did see Vivienne watching Jeb. *What is going on here?* He talked with Jeb for a few minutes and then went to talk to his wife.

"Vivienne, come and walk with me. It is a lovely evening, very warm for this time of the year." She took his arm and he led her into the garden.

"What a lovely party. Jeb seems to be making himself right at home." She stopped to watch the full moon, high in the sky.

"You would know. You have not taken your eyes off him all night. Now what is going on, Vivienne?" She turned to look at him; the moonlight cast a pale glow on his skin. She reached up and stroked his cheek.

"Are you jealous, Abe?" She kissed his cheek.

"Actually I am, but I am also suspicious. Now what are you up to?"

"I am not up to anything."

"I know you Vivienne. You are definitely up to something, now what is it?"

She quickly realized that Abe was not going to let this go. "If you must know, I told Jeb that I would be watching his every move. I don't want him hurting this family and I intend to make sure he doesn't."

"Oh dear, Vivienne, I told you to try to forgive him. Mama is very anxious to have all of us forgive and forget."

"I don't care, I don't trust him. I told him he would have to prove himself and I want him to know that I intend to watch him." She did not mention the threat. "I might have overdone it, but I was making a point. Now, don't fuss over me. I know what I am doing." She walked along the path, her head held high. He hurried after her.

"Don't let Mama or Papa know how you feel. This family has been through enough. They are trying very hard to make him feel like part of this family. He fills the void that Anna left. I mean it Vivienne, do not cause any trouble." She turned and looked deep into his eyes.

"I love you and I love this family, I won't do anything to hurt them. You can relax." Again, she kissed his cheek. "Just know that I would protect you and Eddie with my life." He looked at her and then taking her arm, continued the stroll in the moonlight. They walked in silence, Vivienne was deep in thought. *Don't worry, my Darling. I have taken care of Jeb. He knows what will happen if he steps out of line and I will do what I said. No one will hurt my family, no one.*

Chapter Nineteen

A new business partner

Jeb spent many hours with Jeremy in the export office. He was very knowledgeable about the west and the products that were in short supply. Austin was impressed with Jeb's enthusiasm. "Coal is going to be our most important resource. Union Pacific Railroad has been shipping coal from Carbon, Rock Springs and Almy along the Union Pacific lines for more than 10 years. The Wyoming Coal and Mining Company is willing to work with us and use the Whittakerville depot as a switching yard. This will mean not only will we be shipping and warehousing coal but all of the mining equipment that comes from the east. This is big gentlemen, very big."

One afternoon, he rode out to Isaac's farm. Annabelle was hanging the laundry when he rode up. She waved to him, picked up her basket and walked towards him. She was growing more comfortable with him each time she saw him. Annabelle had completely forgiven Jeb; it was her nature.

"Jeb, nice to see you. Sissy will be thrilled, she has been waiting impatiently for you to visit."

"Annabelle, can I have a word with you before we go and find Sissy?"

"Of course, Jeb. Would you like some coffee?"

"No, thank you. Annabelle, I know that you must hate me for befriending your children and trying to hurt you. I am so sorry. I just want you to know that I would never hurt the children, even back then. I would not have hurt Sissy or Thomas. It was the adults that I was angry with." Annabelle raised her hand to stop him. She could see he was getting very emotional.

"Jeb, I went to church and prayed to God that you would find your place in this family. I have forgiven you, as has Isaac. It is time for you to forgive yourself. I now know that you would not have hurt the children. Sissy is a very good judge of character and she never felt threatened by you, ever." She could see the relief on his face. "I accept your apology for what happened to me. Now please, can we put that behind us? You are Isaac's stepbrother and you are welcome in our home." She extended her hand to Jeb and he shook it gratefully. Just then Sissy bounded from the barn.

"Uncle Jeb, you came. Come on, I will show you the ducks."

Jeb turned back to Annabelle. "Uncle Jeb, I will never be able to tell you how happy that makes me. Thank you Annabelle, you are a good woman. Isaac is a lucky man." Annabelle bent over and wiped Sissy's face with her apron. She smiled as Sissy whisked Jeb away into the barn. She picked up her laundry and walked into the house.

Sissy and Jeb visited the ducks, later they sat beside the pond on the same log that they had sat on long ago. How different he felt now. He felt a special closeness to Sissy. She looked at him with a child's innocence; an innocence that he had never experienced as a child. She chatted about the frogs, the pond, the ducks and the farm. He enjoyed his visit immensely.

Thomas and Isaac arrived within the hour. Jeb and Isaac took a ride out to survey the farm and the two brothers were forming a new bond. Annabelle watched them ride out. *How alike you look, Isaac will be a good mentor for you Jeb.*

Jeremy sat in the study lost in thought. Martha knocked gently on the door before opening it. "Darling, would you like Charles to bring you some lunch?"

He didn't respond. "Jeremy?"

"Oh, Martha. I'm sorry I was thinking. You know I have an idea. Sit down and let me discuss it with you. You know I value your opinion. I always said you have a good head for business." She took one of the large leather chairs in front of his desk, carefully arranging her flowing skirt before sitting. She looked directly at him waiting.

"I am thinking of opening another office. A branch office in Wyoming, in Whittakerville, as a matter of fact."

"Really, and did you have anyone in particular in mind to run this business?" She smiled at him coyly.

"Yes, I am going to ask Jeb, if he would be interested. There is a great deal of money to be made out west. The railroads have opened a huge market to us and we should take advantage of it. What do you think?"

"I think it is a wonderful idea. When will you tell him?"

"I have asked him to stop by after dinner, will you join us?"

Jeb arrived precisely at 7 o'clock. Charles showed him into the parlor. "Martha, Jeremy, how nice to see you. I had a very lovely visit with Isaac's family today." He sat in the chair closest to the fireplace. He was comfortable in this room and both Martha and Jeremy could feel his ease.

"I have a business proposition for you, Jeb." Jeb sat up straighter, focusing his attention on Jeremy.

"You are my nephew and I would like you to head up my new branch office in Wyoming." Jeb was taken aback. He wanted to let Jeremy know of the possibilities in the west but never did he expect this. "It is time that Whittakerville became part of this family's history, a good part."

"I agree, Sir. I am flabbergasted, but truly honored. As mayor of Whittakerville, I am doing all I can to make the town one that you will be proud of." He picked up the brandy that Charles had set in front of him. Swirling the glass, he stared at the amber liquid. Martha smiled; she had seen Jeremy do this many times. "Yes, I would be delighted." He stood and shook Jeremy's outstretched hand. Martha watched with interest. The three discussed the details and over the next week, a plan of action began to take place.

Austin, Jeremy and Jeb spent hours going over the details. All three were very excited about the new offices. Austin agreed to travel to Whittakerville during the next few months to oversee the setting up of the warehousing and the offices.

The entire family was glad that Whittakerville would now hold a happy link for all of them. There was much horror and sadness related to the town, but now perhaps they could begin to more forward. Thomas wanted to know if he could go and visit Jeb sometime. Jeb thought it was an excellent idea.

The day Jeb's train pulled out of the station, most of the family was there to wave goodbye. Vivienne said a polite goodbye and then whispered in his ear, "Don't forget what I said." He looked at her, smiled and whispered back.

"I won't, don't worry. I will not disappoint you." She smiled, in spite of herself.

Austin traveled to Wyoming the following month and was impressed with the new improved town. The train depot was outside of town but it was obvious how it was bringing new prosperity to the town. New construction blossomed along the road from the town center to the depot. He commented to Jeremy that he would not have recognized this as the Whittakerville of twenty years earlier. "It truly is a new improved town, Jeremy. I think the ghost of Jebediah Whittaker is finally put to rest."

Shipments began the next month and the business grew more and more as time passed. Everyone was very pleased, especially Jeremy.

"Martha, we may have lost Anna, but I feel a very close bond with Jeb and it is almost as if he has taken her place. He definitely fills a deep void in my heart."

"No one could ever take Anna's place, Jeremy, but I know what you mean. Isn't it funny how life throws us these twists and turns. Years ago, I never would have believed that I would marry the brother of that horrible monster, yet here we are."

"Yes, my Darling, life is filled with twists and turns, dreams and nightmares. You and I have weathered them all. I love you, Martha." He took her in his arms and kissed her.

"I love you, Jeremy."

Rail travel improved the mail system and letters were exchanged on a regular basis between Jeremy and Jeb.

Dear Jeremy and Martha:

The orders are pouring in from California and Utah. Business is very good. Mining equipment is constantly being shipped. Personal articles including building materials and even whiskey barrels fill the cars. Coal is starting to look like a profitable commodity and we continue to sign more and more clients. The warehouse is filling and emptying on a regular basis and I have hired three more men. The town is booming. We have a new bank, a chemist and second doctor has opened his office here.

On a personal note, Alice Parker is now engaged to our sheriff, Donald Martin. They are a lovely couple. Donald, who never was much of a lady's man, is smitten with her. She is a lovely young woman that is starved for attention but now; she is delighted by Donald's constant interest. I notice that he does not cuss nearly as much. Olga sends her love to Martha.

I trust the family is well, please give them my regards, Although I am keeping busy, I must tell you that I still miss Anna with all of my heart. She would have been thrilled to see the town bustling with new enterprise. I send you all my love.

Your nephew,
Jeb Whittaker, Mayor
Whittakerville, Wyoming

The End

Note from the author:

The Whittaker family has become an integral part of my life. Although this trilogy is now complete, I am going to continue writing about the Whittakers. I shall take individuals and their families and spin more tales of the Whittaker family. I would like to think that my readers would be pleased to continue following their particular favorites.

My next novel, Snow Eagle will be released shortly. We begin another family tale, however this time we are in northern B.C, Alaska and the Yukon with the Tlingit-(First Nations-Native Americans), the time is late 1700's and we meet many new and exciting characters. Watch for Snow Eagle, coming soon.

I love to hear from fans, feel free to contact me through my websites:
www.booksbyshirleyroe.bravehost.com
www.allbookreviews.com

Printed in the United States
152241LV00001B/35/P

9 781849 610094